one

page

love

story

To Sucandhe,
Hope you enjoy the stories!
All the Best,

[signature]

The characters and events that lay within this book are fictitious. The author would like to note, however, that the last time he made such a claim, he received a wonderful Facebook message twelve months later from an equally wonderful girl who described how she had met the love of her life while flying standby to Chicago. All of which is to say that, by suggesting these stories are fictitious, the author only wishes to clarify that he has made them all up. In no way is he hoping to deter you from believing that it is actually possible to meet the love of your life in a pâtisserie in Paris and that it would, in fact, be a great idea to rekindle an old flame within a foggy and silent Times Square. So please, go forth, be inspired by love's many possibilities. Write your own love story. The author would love nothing more than to hear it came true.

ISBN 978-0-9847946-8-3
Also Available in E-book Formats

Cover Design by Cunning Books

Photography by Metroscāp
Front Cover: New York | "Amsterdam"
Back Cover: San Francisco | "Blanket"

Design for Publication by 52 Novels

www.onepagelovestory.com

one page love story

a year in love

love story

Rich Walls

CUNNING BOOKS
New Jersey

Books by Rich Walls

Standby, Chicago
One Page Love Story

To Mom and Dad

IN THIS VOLUME

"If you really love me," she said, *"you'll write me a one page love story."*

And so he did.

FALL

PÂTISSERIE

They met in a pâtisserie beside the Seine. Upon entering, he had held the door for her, saying, "After you," in unmistakable English. To which she replied, simply, "Merci." Now she orders an apple crêpe to complement her morning tea, he a small loaf of bread for his weekend hosts. When she reaches for her purse, he produces a five-euro note, insisting with his very best, "S'il vous plaît." Her acceptance comes in the form of a smile which to him seems by equal weights lovely and strangely familiar. It is at this moment that he wonders whether he should ask this beautiful woman to walk with him, perhaps along the river or down *la rue*. As they exit, however, she turns to him and says, "Don't you remember? We met once, in New York, three, maybe four years ago. You had held the door for me then, too. And what I distinctly remember is wishing that I had asked to walk with you." In a flash, he begins to remember, as well—her and her sun yellow dress awakening that tired, grey morning. "Well," he says, lending his arm, "I suppose this is our second chance."

ALLISON LUCY HEIDLESBURG-LANDIS

Her name is Allison Lucy Heidlesburg-Landis. She's new and from California and Peter has never seen anything like her.

She's tall, maybe five feet already, and tan, like she's come from a place where they even sleep beneath the sun.

And her orange dress! Peter can't remember ever noticing a girl's clothing before, but this! This he notices! It's as if she'd been picked right off the fruit tree by the swings and displayed in front of the black chalkboard like a grand prize.

Or the way she introduced herself using her whole entire name. "Allison Lucy Heidlesburg-Landis," just like that. "Allison Lucy Heidlesburg-Landis," he hears her voice repeating over and over in his head.

He closes his eyes and for a moment thinks he can smell the Pacific Ocean wafting over him from the opposite corner of the room—salty and cool like Heaven. He even brushes his hair back and feels the sea breeze burrow beneath his curly locks.

When he opens them next, Mrs. K is standing beside him.

"Peter, are you okay?" She asks.

"Yes, ma'am."

"Would you like it if Allison sat next to you?" She follows, stepping aside so Allison Lucy Heidlesburg-Landis appears: orange, glowing, magnificent, and holy!

"Absolutely!"

"Very well, then. Have a seat Allison. Peter here will be your class buddy this week."

She sits down and Peter finds himself terrified for the first time in his life by what to say or do next. But as soon as Ms. K turns and asks the class to open their composition books, Allison Lucy Heidlesburg-Landis leans in towards him so closely that her breath puffs against his ears like an actual Pacific breeze, and whispers words that will circle in Peter's mind for years to come:

"Do you like Jolly Ranchers?"

IMPACT

They had been told the asteroid would hit at 5:26 P.M., twelve minutes from now. Yet as they stare into the still lit summer sky, there is no trace of the Long-Island sized rock hurtling in their direction, not yet a single black dot to be found before it might grow to engulf their blue horizon.

The fireworks had been the night before and seen better they had read from Tokyo. Like in the movies, the many heroes had devised a way to send the "wrath of man in the path of God's chosen device." But the result was merely a splintered tail that seemed only to replicate the North Fork from which they now stand.

So at least God kept his sense of humor, they think.

With their final minutes, they gaze into the great blue sky where seagulls dance, inhale the salty air until they become castles themselves, and listen to the rhythm of the waves crashing, foam against their feet. Here, at last, they turn for one another and kiss, feeling the impact of lips meeting forever.

MR. DURBIN

"No, thank you," he replies cheerfully to the pock-faced help, but inside he is disturbed. It takes total concentration, complete focus and silence, even a certain amount of meditation, though he dislikes using that word.

The help disappears and he begins again. Very slowly, very steadily, the lights fade, and soon, like a magician waving his wand, the center tables of the dining area pull away to reveal the glistening wooden dance surface beneath.

As he does this, the many gilded guests enter from the wings like tanned ghosts. Mr. Neaman, his walker gone, struts with the swagger of a collegiate star, Mrs. Neaman beside him, every bit the Homecoming Queen. The DelRay's, the Peacock's, even Louis Habnacker, slender before his years with Linda, playing his natural fool.

Notice the help, moments ago shabby with shirt-tails untucked and poor with black sneakers, now operating the hall in uniforms fit to serve mayors or debutantes—their shirts pressed to a near gloss and shoes that glimmer as they traffic the evening's luxuries. *Coq au vin for you, as well, sir? Why yes, please...*

And as the band launches into its second waltz, bubbling the room like it were the inside of a golden glass of champagne, she enters. Twenty-two tonight, with hair like silk and silver moon eyes against which no chandelier can compete. (No, not even this one that spins just above the joyful dancers' reach.) Yes, she sees him now and she's coming his way! Towards him so close he can nearly remember what it was like to hold her, to close his eyes and feel himself fall like petals to the floor within her scent's embrace...

"Can I get you another refill, Mr. Durbin?"

MISSED CONNECTIONS

My Bus Buddy:

You rode the bus with me every day. For the longest time we never spoke, I even wondered if you knew whether I existed. That is until the day when you asked about the book I was reading (*Still Life With Woodpecker*). I don't think we ever had trouble speaking after that.

Then one day you were gone. First a week passed, followed by an entire month. I was devastated, absolutely certain that I would never see you again.

Until I thought to check the "Missed Connections," and found one titled, "My Bus Buddy," posted every day for three straight weeks, and I knew I had found you.

Two years ago we met for a second time, introducing ourselves and the lives we never knew. This weekend we will marry.

So, to you, with everything I am and everything I believe—thank you for seeking me and finding me. As my wedding promise, you will never miss me again. I am yours to keep.

And to all others—though you may now be missing, until you give up, you have not missed. Your love is waiting. Never, ever give up.

ELIZA

Often times I'll run into old friends, and invariably, after initial talks of business or sports, they'll turn me aside and in a whisper ask, "Whatever happened to Eliza?"

When they do, I offer a lengthy pause, sometimes with a smile which seems to ignite their most eager suspicions, and play a small game with myself, wondering exactly what it is that Eliza might be doing at that very instant. During the day, she would likely be tending her garden or driving towards the village to soak up the local gossip. Or if it is later in the evening, about the time the finer cognacs are delivered, I can reasonably guess that she is upstairs reading to young William.

It's a warm thought, knowing she's doing exactly as she said she would, that she managed to escape to a place where in the evening the sky illuminates brighter than do the streets and where she could marry a man who was rich in his heart and poor in no category but want.

And indeed she did.

I'm not sure why she felt the need to tell me at first, or why she continues to send me her handwritten updates sealed with her lofty "*E.*" Perhaps I help her to remember what it was she escaped. Or maybe she hopes that I, more than the rest, was meant to follow her lead and one day leave the seduction of the city for a life more tame. In full truth, I enjoy the letters too much to ask.

But for them, those who still feel Eliza every time a bar room door opens and a new girl appears, radiating as if someone at the Power Authority permitted a bypass of the whole city grid straight on through her expression, I tell them finally, "I don't know," and I let their imaginations take hold. After all, that's all they were holding on to from the start.

PILLOW

"When did you know you first loved me?" She asks as he slides his hand between the pillow and her cheek. The answer comes to him immediately, though he offers her a thoughtful minute instead, using the time to replay that fateful night in his mind—her making angels in the sand, then cowering from the wind beside the fallen lifeguard's stand. And later as, half-naked and in a fit of panic, she scoured the room for a two-dollar watch which never did glow in the dark. The memory shakes him into an uncontrollable laugh and he falls away from her side. "What's so funny?" She asks now. "I'm serious. I want to know what it was that made you think that I was the one. What was it that made you think that I was the girl you wanted to spend the rest of your life with?" His laughter subsides as suddenly as it began. "You really want to know?" He asks, shifting himself closer again. "Yes," she replies. "Okay, then. August 22nd, 2009," he answers. "You actually know the date?" She cries in disbelief. "How could I not? That was the same night I wondered how I could ever possibly love someone else."

LITTLE BLACK DRESS

You think your little black dress
Could make you forget
That you've made a big fat mess
And you're burning through your boyfriends

You know it's a great big city
They're all so pretty
You let your love get greedy
Now he's gonna find a replacement

So take your little black dress
And try to forget
They won't think anything less
You're just another girl on the pavement

DEAR CINDY

Dear Cindy,

It's 6:21 P.M. on September 27th, 2012. In ten minutes you will officially be one week old.

So, to begin, let me be the first to wish you a very happy one-week birthday. And should you be reading this sixteen years from now, you may care to know that you look absolutely stunning in your Uncle Dave's Marquette onesie. You haven't spit on it even once.

As for the birthday itself, you celebrated well. After a hardy breakfast, you spent your first hour burping to the tune of "Come Together" which made me very happy since we have not yet gotten to that lesson in musical appreciation. At noon, your Grannie and Grandpa arrived and you were every bit the seasoned hostess—wooing them with your irresistible smile and gaga banter. And finally, because the sun still has not rightfully adjusted to you, you are presently enjoying your night's rest, looking every bit the sleeping princess.

Now it is 6:31 P.M. You are officially one week old.

So sleep well, my pretty little Cindy, and dream of the many, many birthdays you are likely to celebrate in fashions even grander than this. But if I can add my two cents, this is the best birthday I've celebrated yet.

Love,
Dad

EVERYTHING TONIGHT

What confounded Thomas was not whether or not he would find love. This he trusted in the same way he trusted that all good things in life eventually will and do work out. No, what confounded him was the fact that she already existed; that at this very moment she was living and breathing, and had been doing so for the same twenty-some-odd years that he had. That she'd grown up and survived grade school, experienced her own first kiss and even first love. Which meant she'd probably overcome heartbreak, too. A love that felt very real on so many levels but inevitably missed on the one or two which make it last. She was out there, on a run maybe, or like him, currently stuck in a grocery line contemplating life's mysteries. And tonight, she would likely be out, as well, updating her status with some silly remark about "Girls Night Out," only to be tagged hours later in a blurry picture with her hand blocking the camera.

What if he were to find her? Tonight. What if he were to be in that picture, tagged right alongside her so that in the morning his friends and her friends would see them together, see that Thomas Oliver is now friends with _____? Would they recognize it any more than he? Any more than she? That the two of them, destined to live a life full of love and joy and triumph, had finally met?

No, it didn't bother him one bit that he hadn't found her yet. After all, you only find her once, and that made tonight worth everything.

PLACE A NOTE ON THE SUN

"I want to try something,"

"Oh yeah? What's that?"

"The sun is just about to set here. What I'm going to do is place a note on it. Just a small one—on the green paper that you like. I'm going to attach it to the sun so that when you wake up you can reach out and it'll be there waiting for you."

"And what's this note going to say?"

"You want to ruin the surprise?"

"I just want to be sure that I pick the right one."

"Fair enough, you make a good point. The one I'm sending will read, 'Good morning honey bee, I miss you, I love you, and I'm on pins and needles waiting for my next chance to kiss you and tell you how beautiful you are.'"

"Ha, very well. Do you think I should send one back?"

"No need."

"Why's that? How will you know that I got yours?"

"It's supposed to rain here in the morning. When I wake up to a blinding daylight, I'll know that the sun saw you so happy that he chased every cloud away to deliver the news."

LET THE LIGHT SOAK IN

The war was neither won nor lost. When it ended it was as if God had simply turned off the rain. The clouds parted and the bullets stopped.

At last they step outside, identifying neighbors who had been no more than moving shadows these last three years. He wonders if his own back crooks the way theirs do now, or if each of his movements ratchet, like a cautious mole, with one foot constantly facing the burrow. How long will that last?

He looks at her, the sun pouring through her skin. He remembers the day they had married, the way the light had bounced off her every feature as if each ray had come in contact with something brighter than itself. But now the light soaks in. There's nowhere else for it to go.

He places an arm around her granite frame.

It's okay, he thinks. Just stay out here for a little while, every day if you need to. Soak it in. Soak it all in until you're so full again that the light dances on your shoulders like it was meant to. Like it always should have been.

STAY UNTIL MORNING

She slides to the end of the bed, tugs her jeans on and reaches down towards where she thinks she left her sweater. It's not there. She wonders if it ever made it to the bedroom at all, even more so when she remembers the voices she heard in the living room before. Had they left?

"Where are you going?" He asks from behind her.

"I was looking for my sweater."

"Does that mean you're leaving?"

"I don't think I should stay."

"Why not?"

"Because."

"Because? That's your answer?"

"Because, why should I? So I can wake up again in five hours and listen to you be nice to me when I know in the back of your mind you're thinking just like I am that this was just fun and we'll both be happier as soon as I'm gone?"

"Okay. But I'm sorry you feel that way."

"Why?"

"Because I like you. Because I had as good a night as I can remember in a long time. And I liked kissing you and to be perfectly honest, I was looking forward to tomorrow, looking forward to being able to kiss you again in the morning, too."

She stands in silence as he continues.

"But if that's the way you feel, your sweater is folded there on the desk. That's where I placed it last night."

THE AGENT BONFIRE

As they watched the embassy burn, illuminating the entire South District like a bonfire set to destroy a decade's worth of misdeeds, they clutched one another.

Only a week before, she'd been a target, a trained assassin. One of Hans Vektor's most trusted agents within his murderous network of killers.

Now they were both dead. Hans literally, his remains blazing within the embassy's cauldron; her figuratively, with her entire history and name smoldering in the same ruins.

She was finally free. Free from the murderous games. Free from the torture. Free from the fear.

She clutched Troy's hand and began to picture a new life ahead of her. Like a phoenix, she would rise from the ashes and begin the life she always dreamed of living.

A bakery perhaps, using her knife skills to cut cakes rather than fingers and an oven's fire to raise bread instead of razing buildings.

She turned to Troy, her newfound hero, her newfound savior. He looked like he'd been through a meat grinder, and in a way, he had.

She found herself reaching for his chest only to recoil at the thought of what she herself had done to it—had been forced to do to it.

Yes, before any of these things, she thought, before any of these dreams, she must first belong to him. Offer him the life he'd given her.

"So you have me," she spoke, "and except for you, I don't exist. In a way, I belong to you right now. What would you have me do?"

"That's right, you're dead right?" He answered with a grin.

"Yes."

"Well, I've never made love to a dead woman before."

THE 5:15

She first started catching the 5:15 three months ago. It was winter then and she'd boarded wearing a parka two sizes too large and cocooned herself in the front car the whole way in. Two days later, she caught on that the regulars always sat in the last car, furthest from the horn along with the best heat, and picked the fourth seat on the right, just behind Frank. She'd been there ever since.

Occasionally, Pete found himself holding longer conversations with Frank, laughing at his exploits, all the while hoping she'd notice how friendly he could be, hoping she might once look towards him, maybe begin to speak to him or offer him her name, but it never occurred. And now he wonders if there's anything he could ever do which would cause her to lower her Kindle and see him as anything more than a train conductor.

That's when he spots her, a red dot in the corner of the parking lot, and a pulse of fear jolts through him. After all his lamenting, he never realized she hadn't boarded.

He leans out and waves her in as she sprints towards him with her purse flailing and red khaki coat stretched like a cape behind her. He'd never held the train before, not for more than a few seconds, at least. But he would hold it for her.

When she's halfway across the lot, white sneakers blurring beneath, he checks his watch—thirty seconds late already with at least fifteen more to go. He'll hear about this for sure.

She wheels closer and for reasons he can't explain (it's totally unprofessional and dangerous if not illegal), he takes a half-step off the train to reach for her like they do in the movies, like they're trained to never, ever do.

She grabs his hand—it's softer than he even imagined—and he pulls her upwards, so quickly that her bag revolves around and cracks the backside of his head as she reaches the top step.

"Thank you," she manages to say through panting breaths.

"You're welcome," he replies as she disappears into the car.

The moment he enters, Frank begins:

"You know Petey Boy, I was late once. Conductor looked me straight in the eye and left without me. Next day I thanked him. That's what the schedule's for. Schedule's there to keep. So tell me, Petey, are we making exceptions now, are we?"

Pete glances towards the next seat, catching her still breathless and watching him with an apologetic smile on her face. He smiles in return, offering her a commonality that had never before existed, and turns back.

"Only for our best customers, Frank."

THE GIRL WHO SAVED THE WORLD

I met a girl once. There was a rumor going around, she said, that she could one day save the world. She never had to, of course, but I kept on believing anyways. After all, that night she had already saved mine.

BAD TAN LINE

The thing was, Jim didn't get it. He never got it. And that was the problem. He would text Ashley and ask her where she was going that night and when she didn't answer he would chase her down from bar to bar, clinging to her like a bad tan line. Even worse, Kyle had begun to notice. And it was driving him away!

Ashley had to do something, something to get rid of Jim. But what? What could she do that would finally get through that thick skull of his? What would get him over this silly fantasy for once and for all?

And then she saw Celeste. Celeste who didn't wear a bra until senior year and even then rarely did just so that boys like Jim would talk to her. That's right, Celeste who had crushed on Jim for every one of the three years Ashley had dated him.

Yes! It was so easy, so blatantly obvious, she had a hard time believing it herself, but Ashley and "Celeste the Pest" were about to become very good friends.

ANYWHERE

"If you could be anywhere in the world, where would it be?" He asks.

She bites her lip for a moment and answers, "When I was younger, I wanted to climb mountains. I always dreamed of what it would be like to be on top of Everest, feeling like you're on top of the world, where sometimes the clouds float beneath you. But that was before I realized I don't like the cold, so now I think I'd like to sail, to be on a boat drifting towards some never ending horizon with no worries at all about where the wind might take me. I think that's where I'd like to be. Why do you ask? What about you? Where would you go?"

"If I could be anywhere in the world," he responds, "it would be right here, beside you. This is where the world slowly floats beneath me and no horizon could ever reveal anything more perfect than you already are."

CUPCAKES AND LOVE

Fill me up, with cupcakes and love
Spin me round, I measure kisses in pounds
And if you feel like I've gotten too skinny
Feed me again, I get fat on your pretty

The scales of love can't hold me up
You've tipped me over with this caramelized crush
Strawberry kisses are for lovebirds dieting
Serve me your sundae with cookies and cream

Oh, your love is sweet
It's a candy cane feast
I don't think I'll ever get full

So please open for me
Your chocolate factory
I found this ticket of gold

Then top all my dreams
With cans of whipped cream
And a cherry for the soul

ECHINACEA LANE

Home seemed further away now, more country-like than I could ever remember. I found her walking Bailey up Echinacea Lane. She was visiting from Philadelphia for her mother's birthday. Life was good, she said, but the hours were tough. It could be worse, though, we both agreed. I asked if she had plans for later that evening and she said that after dinner she did not.

"Amazing how you all have grown up," remarked Mrs. Hines when I arrived at eight. I wished her a happy birthday and we laughed over old incidents while waiting for her daughter to emerge from upstairs. When she did, wearing our old school sweatshirt, Mrs. Hines took a picture.

We decided a walk to the old Summer Swirl would be fitting. She ordered a vanilla cone while I picked mint chocolate chip. Next door, we caught the latest Nick Barrington movie which she had seen before but would not mind seeing again.

Afterwards, I walked her home, all the way back to Echinacea Lane where we passed the empty field lit only by the spotlight moon and silent but for the midnight buzzing of bugs and crickets. Yes, the city felt further than ever now, but those years when we were younger felt closer, and along with it the freedom and tensions of those teenage years seemed more alive.

All that time. Were they opportunities we had missed? Or were we simply too young to know?

I reached my hand out and she took it as we stopped to kiss beside the lit field on Echinacea Lane.

ROUND THE WORLD

Beneath them, the world spun. The Himalayas by day, the Northeast Corridor glowing into the night.

How often they had each dreamt of this view, turned to poets as children—predetermining the loneliness of space, sharing God's vantage point, or, on occasion, humbled beyond words.

But never in their dreaming did they travel as two. Never in all their imaginings did space have room for another.

Yet there she was, right beside him, the revolving sun spinning shadows across the contours of her face.

Suddenly, this mission, "For Benefit of All," seemed to take on an entirely new meaning, one never considered before yet more human than ever. For what benefit could this exploration bring if not to be shared?

As the world spun beneath them, they reached for one another in the weightless space, and kissed.

Above night and above day, over clear skies and cyclones, seven continents and the nearly seven billion of living mankind, they kissed. For one full revolution, ninety minutes, they kissed.

So that the whole world could see, should they look up towards the faint dot now tracing across the sky, that the universe, amongst its infinite mysteries, was a place where love did exist.

Thanks to the kiss spun round the world.

LIKE ATTRACTS LIKE

"If you like to kiss," she told me, "find someone who you enjoy kissing. If you like to dance, find someone who will dance with you even after the band has packed up and gone. Like attracts like, and love lasts a lifetime; pick a love that will like the lifetime spent with you."

THEY MET IN A PARKING LOT

She was crossing the parking lot of SuperValu when he backed his SUV into her. The impact with the bumper dislocated her femur, but it was the fall to the pavement that caused the most damage—two cracked ribs, a shattered wrist, and blunt trauma to her head which resulted in a sixteen-day coma.

He visited each of those days, even stayed most of the nights when no one else would. In pieces, he was able to fill in her background: that her name was Pam and she had moved to town only two months prior. He learned she had a sister in Pittsburgh who was exceedingly nice at first, but after the fifth late night phone call told him that he should move on, explaining it wasn't his fault, that Pam never looked where she was walking. But he stayed anyway. For guilt, for decency, for the woman whom no one else visited.

She woke on a Saturday morning. Three days later came her first words, a stilted and tongue-dry version of, "I'm thirsty," and he returned with a filled jug and extra cups.

In the months to follow, even after she had been discharged, he would continue to fetch her many more waters, many more everything's she wanted or needed.

When she finally asked what she had done to deserve him, he retold the entire story. That it was him that had hit her, that he was only doing what was right.

"No," she responded. "That might have been true at first. But you are still here. That doesn't answer what I've done to deserve your love."

MY FAVORITE PLACE

Two kisses beneath your clavicle. A strange landmark, yet so fragile, with your skin so soft. Tilt my head to reach your lips, or down to where my spirit lifts. A single inch by a single inch, is space enough for me to live. And when I'm gone, this is where I go; for me, this is home. This is where I believe, this is where I dream. This is where I lay myself to sleep. Two kisses beneath your clavicle. A strange landmark, yet so fragile, with your skin so soft.

FALLING LEAVES

When they were children, they used to catch leaves as they twirled to the ground in October. On calm days, she was simply outmatched. He was too fast and the leaves fell too slowly. He reached every one. It was on windier days, though, when a single gust would send dozens of leaves flailing from one corner of the lawn to the other, that she always came out ahead. It was as if she knew which way the leaves would fall.

In marriage, he sensed this was why they had succeeded together so well. His natural abilities could provide for the family through calm years, but whenever a real storm hit—his back injury in 2003, or their cross-country relocation in 2008—he relied on her instincts to guide their family safely through. And she always did.

When her cancer struck, a storm unlike any other, he feared what might await him afterwards. He worried whether he could raise their family by himself without her there to lead them.

"Do you remember that game we used to play," he told her, "with the leaves? It's like the wind's blowing, knocking a thousand leaves down at once, and I'm afraid I won't be able to catch a single one."

To which she replied:

"Be still. That was the key. If the leaf wants to come to you it will. If not, another one will. Remember, there's always another leaf and the game doesn't end when this one touches the ground."

DRUNK TANK

They first met in a drunk tank. He'd been caught urinating on the wheel of a campus security golf cart and she had cold-cocked an actual police officer whom she had wrongly mistaken for an ex.

With the town's second drunk tank under renovation, they were placed together in the same cell where the benefits of their co-habitation were immediate—he held her hair for her as she vomited and afterwards she helped him to aim his pee.

Eventually, she made the first move, sliding onto the two-foot wide bench where they could spoon with her right arm held steady to the floor. Only twenty minutes later, with three squad cars en route filled with half a rugby team, they were unofficially discharged for dry-humping.

It was during their stagger back to campus that he first proclaimed his love to her, explaining that she was indeed the prettiest girl he'd ever met in prison. In response, she asked whether they should both be arrested more often.

Thus, seven years later, as a tribute to that fateful night, and thanks to a not-so-small donation to the local PBA, he arranged to have them both arrested once more in the middle of their class reunion.

As she began to shout vulgar obscenities at the local enforcement from that very same bench, he knelt to one knee and asked if she would be his 'cellmate' forever in marriage.

"Yes," of course, "yes."

THE ONE GIRL AT A BAR THEORY

"Let me simplify it for you," he said. "You don't ever want to have to tell your future wife that she was the second best girl at the bar that night. Pick out a single girl, place her on the pedestal she deserves, and approach her with the confidence of knowing that your heart never settled for anything less."

NEVER PROMISE THE MOON

"I mean it. I love you."

"How much?"

"A lot."

"How much is a lot?"

"A whole lot."

"I want specifics. Do you love me like you just want to get me a purse a whole lot or do you love me like you want to give me the entire world—the sun, the moon, and the stars, a whole lot?"

"Yes. All that. I want to give you the sun, the moon, the stars, and all the planets, and black holes, and Martians, and whatever else is out there. The whole universe. I want to give it all to you."

"Oh my goodness! That's the sweetest thing you've ever said to me. You know that the only thing I ever really need is you, though, right? But since you offered, how about you just get me the purse and we can call the rest of it even."

LONG EXPOSURES

She was a nighttime photographer, traveling from city to city, taking long exposures of their most famous landmarks dressed, as they always are, best at night.

For her New York trip, she had arranged through a friend access to a rooftop on East 36th Street, with the Empire State Building angled to the southwest and the Chrysler Building with its electric crown pointing directly north.

As the friend of a friend supplying the rooftop, he had asked if she would enjoy his company while she worked.

"Sure," she answered. "If you'd like."

And so he sat on a deck chair, sipping from a Six Points, and watched with amusement as she worked her way around the rooftop, stopping only occasionally to inquire about one building or another.

It was not long before he understood her initial hesitation. Photography was a terrible spectator sport. But it was a pleasant evening, and the 42nd story breeze was refreshing after a hot day. He closed his eyes and fell asleep.

By the time he woke again, no more than ten minutes later, it appeared that the girl had gone mad. With a small flash light in one hand, she was twirling in giant loops around the rooftop as part of some bizarre interpretive dance.

"What are you doing?" He asked.

"I'll show you in a minute," she said as she finished her routine with a disco point to the heavens. Afterwards, she unlocked her camera and hopped into the chair beside him.

"I made one for you," she said, handing him the camera.

In the display he saw that above the skyline she had penned the words, "*Thank you*," in light.

"Hit next," she instructed.

He did and saw a different backdrop this time, of southern Manhattan with, "*NYC 2012*," etched alongside the new Freedom Tower.

"Very cool," he said.

"There's one more," she told him.

He hit next one last time and began to laugh aloud.

"Absolutely," he responded as he composed himself to her final picture, of midtown Manhattan and the message she had written in the city lit sky:

"*Buy me a drink?*"

FOREVER IS HALF ENOUGH

"What surprised you the most?"

"How quickly it went. I remember when I first proposed to Grace. At the time, spending the rest of my life with her sounded so enormous, almost infinite. I think what has surprised me most is how quickly it's passed. How very finite the time I spent with her got to be. Fifty-five years. To some people that's an eternity. But not to me. I could spend another fifty-five years with her and it wouldn't be half enough. Not half enough at all. Unless you gave me forever, though! Forever might be half enough."

ON FLATULENCE

She farted. Not loudly or altogether noticeably, but she had farted. On the Richter Scale of Flatulence it might have only been a 2, but it had sent a distinct vibration across the stretched fabric of the couch.

He wondered if he should acknowledge it. On one hand, it might serve to progress their relationship. After all, the couple that farts together stays together. On the other hand, though, he had to consider that the mere suggestion of having noticed could very likely revolt or terrify her— the implications of either reaction being disastrous.

The stench began to waft over. The culprit was easy to pinpoint: this morning's eggs benedict strengthened by the toxin of three mimosas. Also, perhaps, the leftovers of a Cobb salad at lunch. It was a nasty, filthy thing and he admitted to himself that he was impressed.

He did not move until after the cloud had passed because he feared that any movement would implicate her. When he did spy over, her eyes were planted on the TV with no expression. Was it possible that she had not even noticed?

No, he decided. That was decidedly impossible.

So he leaned over, kissed her beside the temple, and did the only act justifiable in this situation—he unleashed the storm cloud of gas that had been ravaging his insides all evening long.

OUR STORY

Though I know there are more romantic stories of young couples swept off their feet, or more arresting stories of love at first sight, our story is a little bit simpler, a little more grounded. In short, in a time of crisis, she was there for me, and when she needed a miracle from me, I was prepared to deliver one for her.

SUPERHEROES AND BALLERINAS

He was Awesome Man, with Rubbermaid gloves and a flannel cape. She was a ballerina, a tutu puffed about her hips. And I believed it. That he could save the world and she could within a twirl reveal its beauty. For certain, they believed it, the way they fell into character as they dashed about the street with arms held forward to fly or peaked above her head to spin. And you should believe it, too, for one day the world will be in need of a hero or an absolute example of beauty, and whether they exist may very well depend upon if you found a Snickers too steep a price to pay for their dreams tonight.

NO SHOT

Dear Kate,

Though this will likely seem off putting and will likely kill any chance of securing a second date with you, given my low odds already, I thought it worth the shot.

Quite simply, I am terrified by you. Like on a gorgeous scale of "1" being your typical hot and "10" being Jennifer Aniston-squared, you are a thousand.

As a result, and despite my best efforts, I completely and totally couldn't say a normal thing to you tonight even though on the inside I thought it was really cool that you're connecting your students with that class in China and that *Groundhog Day* is one of my favorite movies, too.

In short, I am not a mute. I just wasn't expecting to be set up with someone as pretty as you.

Sincerely,

Josh

P.S. Sorry also about the spilled wine.

WHAT DID YOU WANT TO BE?

"What did you want to be when you grow up?" He asks. "Well first I wanted to be a princess," she says, "and then I wanted to be a singer, to be in the spotlight, belting my heart out in front of packed arenas. Once, for an entire week, I thought I wanted to be a paleontologist, digging gigantic dinosaur skeletons out of the ground; or a scientist, playing with microscopes and beakers and being the one to discover how the world works. Then a doctor to help people, a vet to help animals, a teacher, to show kids how the world works...Basically, at one time or another, I've wanted to be just about anything you could ever think of. Why do you ask? What did you want to be when you grow up?" "For as long as I've known, I've only wanted to be with you."

TRASH BAGS

I am handed a bulging trash bag and told to organize its contents. Afterwards, I can take the neat piles down the hall where the larger organized piles are being held. Simple enough. This makes me a good person.

I rip the bag open and blindly dig my hand in, feeling strangely embarrassed as my hand burrows between cotton articles, the same way I am embarrassed to pull another person's laundry from a dryer. I remind myself that these are donated. At this moment, they belong to no one.

The first item is a sweatshirt. Billabong, blue with yellow stripes. It is Children's size and I place it on the floor, mindful to mark that space as Children's.

Next is a large green windbreaker. Baltustrol. I create a new Men's pile.

A second sweatshirt. It is white except for where it reads, *Camp Ivanhoe 2006*. Children's grows by one.

Sweatpants next: Victoria's Secret PINK brand. They seem small enough for a child, but then I remember my girlfriend's clothes always appear small, too. I stand in the hallway, lifting the PINK pants for seven seconds before I decide they belong in a Women's pile. I am again embarrassed.

Camp Ivanhoe 2009. Green this time and slightly larger than 2006's. He must be in high school by now.

Girls' jeans makes a Girls' pile. A New York Giants jacket creates a jacket pile. A unisex Myrtle Beach sweat-shirt adds to Men's.

Aéropostale, J. Crew, Champion, Abercrombie, Nike. Stone Harbor, Hannah Montana, Race for the Cure, Lehman Brothers.

These are all pieces. Together, I can nearly picture them: a family of four. They met at Scranton, raised two kids in Jersey, and spend their summers down the shore. The boy, a senior, plays third base; the girl, finishing middle school, sings. During the day, Dad works in finance while Mom teaches.

And they give. They remembered to give.

Inside this bag are my neighbors. Pictures would do, but there's more than one way to tell a story. Here are the clothes they picked out. Here are the clothes they grew up in. Here are the clothes they chose to give away.

Outside, in a short line around the block, are the recip-ients, families whose lives have woven in a vastly different direction. Soon these clothes will become their story.

The trash bag is empty now. I have six neat piles. There are fifty more bags waiting. With help, I will organize those, too. For there are fifty more stories, and it is cold out, and the clothes will keep them warm and by tomorrow the floods will have receded completely and the sun will come out and we will all move on, because we are good people. And good people move on.

LOVE VOTES

Love votes. It elects every day those who we believe in, who we are inspired by, and who we would endanger ourselves to protect. It sits not idly on the sidelines, indifferent to its leanings, nor will it allow itself be spoken for. Love has a voice, a voice that speaks loud and clear. It says I am here today and I will place my faith for tomorrow in you. What other choice could there be? None, if it's a love that's free.

Love votes. Do you?

MAKES US FOOLS

Oh, love is magnificent
Oh, love is true
It makes you weak
It makes us fools
I was walking by the water
Last Wednesday about eight
You saw me with another girl
Then you pushed her in the lake
Oh, love is mysterious
Oh, love is true

It makes me weak
It makes us fools
You were out in the country
Just north of Buck's Head
I saw you with another boy
Then I shot him in the leg
Oh, love is miraculous
Oh, love is true
It makes us weak
It makes us fools
You brought me into the city
Took me here on this date
I saw you poison my whiskey
Just kiss me 'fore it's too late

LONG PAUSES

"Hey sweetheart." "Hey." "How's everything back home?" *"Good." "How did your dentist appointment go?" "No, that's tomorrow." "That's right." "How was your meeting?" "It went well. They liked my idea on the Green Square project." "You were working hard on that." "…" "…"* "There's a great sushi place across from the hotel. I think you would like it." "Really? That's nice." "…" "…" "And, it was funny, today, I took a cab and told the driver 8*th** and Market by accident. I wasn't thinking. But it turns out there's an 8*th* and Market here, too." "Ha. That is funny." "…" "…" "What's that?" "What's what?" "That noise." "Oh, I'm baking cookies for Henry's class." "That's nice of you." "…" "…" "Listen, you don't always have to call. I'll be okay. We're doing fine here. It's just that I just don't want you to feel like you have to." "But you know I like to." "I know, I just don't want you to—" "Kate?" "Yes?" "Can

I tell you something I've never told you before?" "What's that?" "Fourteen years ago I made a promise to myself that I would spend every night by your side. When I realized I had to break that promise, the next best thing was to make sure that every night I hear your voice, no matter how little we have to say. So this is me promising to you that I will always call." "…" "Are you there? Is that enough?" "It's everything, John. It's everything."

FIRST KISS

There was a picture of them, from twenty-four years earlier, of he the ring bearer in a svelte black suit and she the flower girl in a pink dress that puffed as wide as she was tall. They had never met before that day and would not meet again until they reached college. Neither remembered one another, or much of that day altogether, but soon they found themselves in love.

Several years later, and exactly four days after sending out the invitations, she received a phone call from her Aunt Lynn. "How long have you known each other?" Aunt Lynn asked. "Since college," she replied earnestly. "Oh boy," answered her aunt. "Do I have a surprise for you."

The following weekend Aunt Lynn arrived with her wedding album, a massive thing weighing close to twenty pounds and taking up half the coffee table, and opened to a saved place smack dab in the center where a single photo took up a whole page:

Of him in his svelte black suit and of her in her wide pink dress; the two of them holding hands as he placed a puckered kiss on her smiling cheek.

Yes, their first kiss had been long before she ever imagined.

TIMES SQUARE

In twelve years here, he had never seen a fog so thick. The high definition video boards lining Times Square were reduced to an indistinguishable light show, faint colors pulsing through the gray.

She arrived at 7:17 a.m., only two minutes late, appearing like a mirage so that one second he was entirely alone, the next she was there with him.

Her hair was shorter now and he caught himself placing a hand to it. She did not shy away, only looking at him with a peculiar glare as he glanced his finger tips over the soft strands that ended at her chin.

For a moment he thought he might have formed words enough to make a sentence, but the phrase he had come up with seemed to disappear like he feared she might, back into the mist, back into another city, lost for two years or more again.

So he lowered his hand to her hip and held her so she could not go. He was glad when she did not resist and even felt himself tremble when she placed her own hand over his.

Comforted, his mind wandered again. How strange, that Times Square could be tamed like this—the fog blanketing the lights, the holiday tempering the traffic's normal din, and having her, here, alone with him.

How strange indeed. The very center of the modern world hushed for the moment that they could meet again. Intimate in the place where intimacy is lost.

THE WOMAN IN RED – PART I

A man approached a woman in red at a bar.

"How do you know that I am not already with someone?" She asked.

"I do not know," he answered.

"But yet you would risk it to talk to me—the embarrassment and perhaps jealously that might tear at you should a friend of mine arrive?"

"It would be worth that risk," he said.

And sure enough, her companion arrived, and the man felt both embarrassed and jealous.

THE WOMAN IN RED – PART II

Two hours later, the woman in red approached the man.

"You stayed," she said.

"I stayed," he replied.

"And why would you stay when it is clear that I have my company for the night and you have clearly deemed no other woman worthy? Was the embarrassment not enough?"

"I have stayed because you have not yet left. When you have done so, I will accept that it is time to leave, as well. Until then, I will wait."

And the woman turned for her companion and left.

THE WOMAN IN RED – PART III

The man stayed at the bar longer still. No longer embarrassed and no longer jealous. He had found companionship in the night itself—his scotch, the faces, and a phrase that seemed to repeat itself over and over in his only slightly-drunk mind. "No, love is not to be feared," he thought. "Not to be feared at all."

And the woman in red returned, sitting down beside him.

"You lied," she began. "You said you would leave when I had left."

The man turned to her and said, "The night is not nearly over yet and you are here now. Therefore, you have not really left at all.

"But," he continued before she could speak, "I am tired. So with your forgiveness, I must ask if you are now prepared to leave."

When she answered, "Yes," they both stood, and offering his arm, the man exited the bar with the woman in red.

SEVEN MINUTES

When he closed the door he found her in the far corner of the small square space, with thin slits of light from the outer basement drawing lines across her shins. Her hands were pressed backwards and thumbed blindly between the shelves of folded linens.

He made a cautious move to join her, stepping to the opposite corner where his nervous hands found the shelves filled with board games instead.

"We don't have to do this," he whispered, mindful that the basement had reached a disturbing level of quiet which screamed of open ears.

She did not respond, only gazed towards him, her eyes reflecting a pool of light which could not exist.

"I've never kissed a girl, either," he continued. "So it's okay. We can sit if you want."

And he sat down, with his knees bunched close to his chin, hoping that she would take this as a sign of peace, anything that might calm her nerves even as his own seemed to vibrate beneath his skin.

"You never kissed a girl?" She said at last, still standing.

"Nah," he responded.

"Well, did you ever *like* a girl?" She asked, squatting now so her eyes were level with his.

"Yeah."

"Then why didn't you kiss her?"

"Embarrassed, I guess."

"You should have. She would have liked it."

Nervously, he looked towards the floor, where the slits of light began and instinctively followed each of them up like a ladder to where the last now crossed the very base of her chin. She had a small freckle there, and for reasons yet unexplained to him, but perhaps better known to adventurers and seafarers who can readily spot amongst constellations of many or a few that single star by which to lay their dreams upon, he knew this had been his.

He leaned forward, his hand crossing the illuminated threshold, and stopped with his face held a mere breath away from hers.

"Do you really think she would have liked it?" He asked.

"Yes," she responded.

And, amidst the folded linens and board games, heaven was theirs.

OBITUARY

DIED, HANK PETERSEN, ONE WEEK AFTER PASSING OF ELEVEN-TIME WIFE

Hank Petersen, 93, of Sleepy Hollow, NY, died Thursday following complications of a recent illness. His passing came exactly one week after the death of his eleven-time wife, Eleanor Petersen. The couple, first married in 1941, divorced a total of ten times—most recently in 2002. After a six-month separation, they remarried for the eleventh and final time in January, 2003. In a February 9, 2003 article for the Daily Reporter, Mr. Petersen remarked that while "we were never really very good together, we were even worse apart." Mr. Petersen is survived by three children, Hank, Jr., Joseph, and Diane, as well as their eleven grandchildren. All three children are currently enjoying their first marriages.

MINGLERS

"Well, the funny thing was that we were both on online dates when we met. He had picked this red headed girl, Alice, off of Mingler and my date was this really nice guy named Kyle that I found on Frisky Frisco...yea, I know...but seriously, don't laugh until you've looked...anyway, completely random, both our dates happened to be at L'Etoile, and we're seated right next to each other, still having never met, and I don't know who overheard the other first, but somehow we figured out that everyone's on a first date, and it's still in that sort of awkward stage, so we decided to pool together and made a night of it. Well by the time we hit the second bar, Kyle was nearly ready to propose to Alice already while Dan and I were trying to figure out the most polite way to excuse ourselves so we could go home and make out. Long story short, in June we're going to Alice and Kyle's wedding, and in July you can meet them at ours..."

UNTIL YOU MEAN IT

"I lo—"

"Wait," she said. "Not yet. Don't say that yet. That's something I've heard too many times before only to find it had meant the wrong thing or something else. 'I love you, but—.' I don't want that with you. And I don't want to put you under any pressure either, where you feel like you have to say it. Because it's okay. If right now you only like me a lot and maybe one day that grows into love, that's good, too, I'm happy to wait. I will wait for you as long as it takes. But just please, the one thing I ask, is please don't use that word until you mean it. Until you're absolutely sure, when you absolutely believe beyond a shadow of a doubt that I'm the one who will make you happy and that I'm the one who can make your life complete. But not until then. Because love is the one word you can't take back."

"Okay. But will you do one thing for me?"

"Of course."

"I want you to hold my hands, look me straight in the eyes, and believe me when I say, in every connotation, that I love you."

HAPPY THANKSGIVING

Jim sat on a deck chair, one of the few pieces of working furniture he still owned, and stared in disbelief at the simmering heap that had been his house. Jill had left for her parents two hours earlier with the girls, leaving Michael with him to bounce around the ruins.

Where was Michael? A quick panic woke him from his daze to find Michael, hockey stick in hand, turning over smoldering items from the outskirts of the wreckage.

"Be careful!" He thought to yell, but on what authority? Certainly his son hadn't been the one to burn down the family house on Thanksgiving. That badge honor now belonged solely to him.

"Twenty-four hours, you've got to let it thaw for twenty-four hours," he heard his co-worker reminding him earlier that week. So what if he had gotten home late from work and forgotten to take the turkey out until the children had gone to bed. So what that he had just left the garage and entered the kitchen when the bird exploded...

For the first time, he began to cry. It was like the hydrant from earlier pouring out from him. What if one of the kids had been in there? What if Jill had been in there? And all of their belongings, all of their memories. Eight years of building a family here. He'd wrecked it all. On the whim of trying something new, he'd burst it all in flames.

"Dad!" Michael was sprinting towards him.

"What's going on, Michael?" He asked, wiping his eyes.

"Everything else is burnt to a crisp, but look what I found!"

It was a family portrait, only slightly charred on the edge of the frame, taken in the Bahamas last February. Jill, Gracie, Katie, Michael, and him.

"Happy Thanksgiving, Dad."

WICKED GIRL

Once upon a time there lived a wicked wench of a girl. Everywhere she went she would hurl her vitriol at the nearest and most willing male victim, cascading him with a waterfall of verbal punishment meant to destroy every leg of pride he was ever born with. That is, until one day, an old maid who was once quite awful herself, placed a spell onto her by which the next man the girl were to meet, whether handsome or vulgar, would only hear sweet nothings pour from the lips of her mouth.

As it happened, the old maid lived near a family of goat herders, amongst which included a single son named Pubis. Pubis was young indeed, barely sixteen, and bulbous, round and as fat from every limb as a bloated cow. Being a goat herder, and a rather unhygienic one at that (using the same brush on himself as on his goats), he smelled something ungodly, which is to say nothing of his own speech—stunted to the level of a six-year old and showing clear favor for the word, 'shitbiscuit.'

So as they passed, young Pubis, with a pimple the size of a goat's hoof ogling like a third eye from the center of his forehead, looked at the girl and said, "Aw, shucks, see you almost stepped in that shitbiscuit!" To which the girl thought to reply, "Well it'd be better than having my foot graze the dung-pile that you are!" Only, rather, the words that came from her mouth, to Pubis's adolescent shock were, "Well I'd been so blinded by your handsome self, I nearly lost my proper step."

And as she heard these words emitted by her own true voice, the wicked girl coiled in a fear she had never known…

THE HIGHWAY

She looked towards him, his attention held steady on the road, then down, where his hand locked with hers beneath the radio. She wondered if he knew where they would end up, if he saw something in the darkness ahead, a special place they might soon reach, or whether he was simply counting the dotted lines as they blazed by underneath, relieved by the thought of leaving each one of them behind.

She turned backwards in her seat. In the far distance were the dual headlamps of a tractor-trailer. Much further behind was home where she had left a short note for her parents, "Gone for a long drive, please don't call, I will be back in a few days."

Of course they had called and she had placed her phone on silent. She knew they would go ballistic, that they had every right to, but she also knew that that time was not now and it would not be anytime soon.

She faced forward again, followed the invisible line from his eyes towards the furthest illuminated point in the road and felt an eagerness rush through her. Yes, they would do this. They would keep going so far as they could. Because this was the dream, just as it was intended. This is why the highway existed: for them, for love, for never stopping.

And the highway would not stop for a very long time.

Q&A

Q: How do you write a love letter?
A: One word at a time.

A MOUSE IN LOVE

Once upon a time there was a mouse in love. This may seem strange to you, that a mouse could be in love, but consider the vantage point of the mouse, who by equal measure, thought it quite silly himself that humans could love, they always being so busy with other things. But love this mouse did, more so than any other activity that filled his days—more than he ate, more than he slept, and more than he roamed the cavernous city you call New York. More than any of these things, most of all, he loved.

So please, pay heed, next time you cross paths with a dizzy mouse. For it may not be that he is merely dizzy to eat, nor dizzy to sleep, but rather, much like you, simply dizzy in a dream. Dreaming of the mouse he loves.

RETIREMENT DINNER

...And finally, it's funny, I look around the room, see so many leaders, other chief executives, a few congressmen, Senator Hall here...How are you Frank? Do we need to get you a few more rolls? Leaders...surrounded here by leaders, and when I look back on my career, I think that was my single defining goal, or trait—to lead. Not to become the CEO of a great multinational, or to become one of the world's most powerful businessmen, but to lead on a daily basis. I always believed in myself, and I always believed I knew what was right, or at least closest to right, and I knew if I could lead others to do the same, to inspire them to lead using their own remarkable talents, that we would be successful. And we have been.

But now that my work here is nearly done, and I've the chance tonight to thank the so many of you who have entrusted so much to me, allowed me to be your leader for what seems to have been such a short period of time, perhaps it's now safe for me to admit the one place I did not lead, but followed instead.

My wife, Anne.

Anne, in everything I've done, in every place I've wanted to go in life—it was in your footsteps. You are my moral compass, my strength when difficult days left me with little or none left, and always my hope that tomorrow will be better. I will follow you so long as I live, and I cannot thank you enough for allowing me to be by your side throughout this great, long journey. So thank you Anne— with 50,000 employees, our thousands more shareholders, and most everyone else in this room, all still following me for at least another fourteen hours or so—let me finish by saying that it's been the absolute privilege of my life to follow you.

SHINE

Lift up a piano
Fold it like loose leaf
Toss it from a rooftop
Toss it from your mind
You have an umbrella
With holes poked inside
You felt it on your forehead
Will you feel it where you rhyme?
Stars will shine on their own
And it's known that you can shine
For once forget the moon
And shine, shine, shine
I'll be here waiting
I've unwrapped the keys
I don't mind the rain
But I'll always need your light

PRINCESS

She allowed her daughter to help pick out her dress. First it was the gold one from 1998 that she never could throw away. For Mia's sake, she squeezed into it, looking ridiculous. But of course, when she stepped out, Mia went slack-jawed at all the gold and sparkling.

"You look just like Belle!" Mia squealed.

She told Mia to pick out two more. In one she looked like Ariel, the next, Cinderella. Soon it was getting late, though, and she needed something she could actually wear.

Together they settled on the Vera Wang knock-off she had bought for Tracy's wedding in 2010. She was disappointed at what only two years had done to the fit, but was comforted by Mia's insistence that she was still the prettiest girl she had ever seen in real life.

Though she knew Mia would hop out of bed to watch shows with Grammie the moment she left, she tucked her in anyways and told her that she would make a fine princess one day before kissing her goodnight.

Finally set to leave, she paused at the mirror by the front door and willed herself to enjoy the night ahead. Yes, tonight would be a good night she told the mirror twice. And this time she really was ready, ready to try again. Surely even a Disney Princess would be given a second chance.

THE HONEYMOONERS

It was okay now, Mack thought. For one, they would be safe here. The zombies couldn't access the rooftop and they had exit points on two sides if necessary. But more importantly, with the group fast asleep, he finally had time to run over the event that had haunted him all day long but which he refused to allow himself to consider until they were totally secure for the night. Until now.

He began to run through the hundreds of other kills he had tallied, whether he'd ever seen anything like it—two zombies coordinating. The closest he could remember had been in Norwalk. Those two had jumped out of a shed and Mack had nearly got himself killed hesitating over the idea that the attack had been orchestrated. It wasn't until Holcomb had saved his hide with a sledgehammer that Mack realized the tandem had actually been a pair of conjoined twins in their prior lives—literally tied at the undead hip.

That was it, though. The only instance he could come up with. In each and every other attack the zombies had acted independently of one another. Sometimes they moved in packs, for sure, but that was like watching gnats swarm towards light. Up until today, he was certain of the fact that when jaws came to blood, it was every zombie for itself.

Up until today, he thought again. Up until the honeymooners (The fact he'd already nicknamed them only seemed to solidify his suspicions.). As soon as he raised his machete, one of them actually *dove* in front of the other, sacrificing itself in the process. And then, the image he couldn't shake, was her, no *it*, he had to correct himself, it, it, it…staring down towards her former lover, seeing the remains of his zombie-corpse writhing on the ground, and turning back towards Mack with all the rage of a love-scorned bride.

No. Zombies weren't supposed to love. They weren't supposed to love at all. And the fact that the honeymooners did love scared the crap out of Mack.

INCOHERENT

"Excuse me, Simon, do you have a moment?"

"Yes, Mrs. Gilbert?"

"I was wondering if you could explain this."

"What's the matter?"

"The assignment was to write a love poem."

"But I did write a love poem."

"Simon, writing is an expression of your thoughts, it should be coherent."

"I'm sorry, Mrs. Gilbert, but since when was love coherent?"

IT WILL BE OKAY

"I saw a young couple on the train the other day, they couldn't have been more than seventeen, and not only was the girl crying, but it was clear that the boy had been, too. He had his arm around her and seemed to be doing all the right things to try and cheer her up but it just struck me at the time as so unbelievably sad. Kids these days, they're so good at bottling up their emotions, to see them pouring out in public, it really made me want to reach out and help them. But I also knew you can't do that. You can't always be that old stranger on a train helping every person with every little problem. That's one of the sweet joys of life—triumph or tragedy—we get to figure out all these things on our own. We get to learn and grow, mature and develop at our own pace. So knowing this, that I would be forced to let them be, I suddenly couldn't help but feel this absolute overwhelming sense of beauty, how beautiful it was that at this very despondent time in their young lives, these two had one another. And this peace, giddiness really, flushed right through me, and even though I knew I would never say a thing, I felt my insides just screaming to share with them that, 'It will be okay, for both of you. As long as you keep one another, as you are now, life will be okay.'"

EMERITUS

Delivered May 14, 2012, by former Dean Nubert:

I wonder, do any of you realize just how close to we are to The End? Imagine locking lips with the co-ed next to you and then opening your eyes to find the Grim Reaper glaring down at your pimpled face. That's how close we are. And yet you're still sitting here, prepared to listen to a middle-aged man spout false truths while you chew gum. We may as well drop the bomb now...My generation's failed you. Our single success was to speed up the ways in which we destroy one another. Now if you need a war, you just press a button. Want a financial meltdown? Press a button. How about a sex change operation? Press a button. That's a good one: values. What about values? Social values. Do you even know what those are? That's a rhetorical question by the way. I want you to look around—have you ever heard that before, look left and look right? Well I want you to look to your left and then to your right— chances are that one of you will end up divorced, two of you will be laid off at some point, and the third, despite your brave commitment to your marital vows and a penchant for working well past midnight, you'll still wake up one day morbidly obese and clinically depressed. Yes, but at least you'll have all those anniversaries to look forward to…That's what we've left you with…Do any of you wonder what it all means? What's the point? As we obliterate ourselves back to the Stone Age, I'm beginning to think perhaps our Neolithic ancestors had it right. Survive and reproduce. That's it. I bet we could even consider that as a motto here. What do you think, Paul? Think we can find the Latin equivalent for 'Survive and Reproduce,' ad infinitum? No? Maybe not…But I suppose that's my advice for you here today, or the best I've got anyway. First, learn how to survive as if this were the arctic winter and there was but one buffalo to split amongst all twelve-hundred of you. Yes, that'll teach you how to survive quickly. And secondly, and I'll bet this will really galvanize your sordid little minds, reproduce. That's right, [expletive deleted] like rabbits. As many times as you can and with whomever you can find. Use love as an excuse if you have to. I did. More than once. Didn't I Professor Olson? That's right, make as many of you as you can, because Lord knows we as a species probably won't last, but wouldn't it be fun to stand in line at the pearly gates and notice that the last twenty in line all have your face?

[End of Transcript]

LITTLE PIGGY

This little piggy went to the market,
This little piggy went home.
This little piggy had roast beef,
This little piggy had none.

And this little piggy…this little piggy…well, this little piggy went on the greatest adventure of his life. He sailed across the widest seas, climbed the highest mountains, rode a rocket ship into space, and fell back to the earth with the biggest parachute ever made. He crossed the Sahara and even traveled the entire length of the Amazon. He did all of these wonderful things, until one day, he received a letter by courier, postmarked from Peoria, Illinois, asking for him to return. And for the first time in three years, this little piggy's hooves stopped dead in their tracks. From the base of that volcano he realized the happiest days of his life had been the ones he had spent back in Peoria, with his sweet, sweet, Lilly. Well, do you know what this little piggy did next? He picked himself up, politely thanked his guide, and began racing eastward, as fast as his hooves could speed him, going WEEEWEEEEWEWEEEWEWEWEEEEEEEE all the way home!

WENDY

Wendy and I had corresponded for several weeks before we met, she always sending and ending her messages with the same

Warm Regards,
W.

In that time, I had established a near complete image of her in my mind: petite, intelligent blonde hair, a dimpled cheek that might turn rose in the cold, and a countenance which, and perhaps this was asking too much, might remind me of what it's like to see someone and feel completely reassured that this is where I most belong.

It was a pleasant image, comforting in that sepia, candlelit tone that somehow turns an event you've been looking forward to into something altogether nostalgic, as if life were about to hand you the very thing you presumed to have been lost forever.

I was sure of it, that she would be the piece of me that I'd been missing.

And then she entered the restaurant. Her cheeks were rosy, in fact, so red that they seemed to make the cold itself blush for its impact, but there the comparisons ended. Had I known earlier how limited my imagination could be…or perhaps those are the types of games we love to play, after all, no other desire lacks so little in imagination as does hope…but in reality, there was no way of knowing. In every way, she was more than I could ever imagine.

KISSING SQUARE

T.M. + W.O.
HERE ON 12/07/03
KISSED 2HR 27MIN
BEAT THAT!

DINER

The diner was nearly empty when Delores sent Jo Ann home early. The last wave had come and gone and she could easily serve those who were left—two night patrolmen sipping coffees at the bar seats, some high school kids lingering over ice creams, the Dylan's with their nightly soup, and finally, the man and woman sitting with their backs to one another in booths 24 and 26.

Delores had never seen either before, but she approved of each immediately. The woman, pretty and professional, had been exceedingly apologetic when she ordered only a hot tea for herself. As for the man, he was equally handsome and had brought a better appetite—ordering a western omelet, a side of bacon, and a decaf coffee to wash it all down.

She approximated them to be near the same age, likely thirty-one or thirty-two. More importantly, a pair of refills proved their ring fingers to be bare. Perhaps they would find it out of place to discover their waitress playing matchmaker, but she would pay no mind. At this hour, this *was* her place, and to Delores, sitting alone in a booth at midnight was decidedly far more out of place.

Between the man and the woman, booth 25 remained open. There she placed three slices of pie alongside two waters. She then prepared both of their checks without being asked and made her move.

Handing the checks to each, she said, "There is someone I would like you to meet, and if you would just take a seat in the booth behind you, perhaps you will find it worth your while."

In each instance, they circled their heads around as if being played for a TV stunt. When they caught eyes for the first time, however, Delores knew she had them hooked. He stood first and sat down in the booth as if being directed. The girl lingered longer (Delores thought she might have to kick her after a minute), but soon enough succumbed and made a shy twirl around the divider, sitting at the very edge of the seat biting her lip.

An hour and a half later, like the patrolmen at the bar, the high school kids up front, and even the Dylan's with their soup, the three slices of pie had disappeared, but the man and the woman in booth 25 remained.

THIS IS US

This is us. This is us doing the best we can. It may not always look pretty, but we are trying, every day. And we'll keep on trying, right on through the end. That's the one thing we've always been good at. And who knows where this will lead, if after all our mistakes we'll have learned anything new, but we are going to keep living, and I promise you, we'll keep loving all the way through.

This is us, and I think we're gonna make it. I hope you do, too.

WINTER

ROMEO LIVES

Apparently Romeo hadn't died. Hadn't died at all. Rather, when Juliet bent down to kiss his poisoned lips, Romeo grasped her with all the intent of a warm-blooded teenager suddenly given a green light for some highly dramatic P.D.A.

By the time Mr. Thompson stumbled into the scene from stage left, Romeo (or Chuck Olhoff to be more precise) had his hand halfway down Monica Mendez's bodice while she seemed nearly ready to unsheathe a far different dagger than Juliet's fatal tool.

Then, in perhaps one of the most daring revisions in the play's history, a gang of three Capulets and two Montagues rushed the stage, tackling Mr. Thompson before he could reach the star-crossed lovers. As he hopelessly writhed to wrestle free, and Chuck and Monica continued their passionate twist, the Prince entered from stage right:

A glooming peace this morning with it brings;
The sun, for sorrow, will not show his head:
Go hence, to have more talk of these sad things
Some shall be pardon'd, and some punished:

"Including you Mr. Westby!" Shouted Mr. Thompson.
For never was a story more dope
Than this of Monica and her Chucky-O!

A STRANGE REQUEST

"This might sound a little strange," he said, *"but if I told you right now that I really* like you, but if I also asked that instead of acting on it, could you be my friend first? I just have this feeling that sometimes, and eventually, you need to find that soul mate or lover or whatever you want to call it, but that other times, what you need more is a really good friend. And I didn't want to hide it anymore, the fact that I really, really like you, but I also know that's not exactly what I need right now. I just kind of need you, here."

"It's not strange," she answered, knowing exactly what he meant. "I'll be whatever you need me to be, and I'll always be here for you."

THE RE-RUNS

You just got home
I've got the TV on
Yes, I've seen this one before
We are so young
We should be having fun
And I don't want to become a re-run

This dinner's great
Our knives can scratch the plate
Yes, I've seen this one before
We are so young
We should be having fun
And I don't want to become a re-run

I hear the laughing track
When we hit the sack
Yes, I've seen this one before
We are so young
We should be having fun
And I don't want to become a re-run

KNOCK KNOCK

"Knock knock."
"Who's there?"
"The man."
"The man who?"
"The man who's pinching himself right now, wondering if it's actually possible that he's woken up beside the single most beautiful woman he's ever seen. Yes. It must be. Because I know I don't have half of the imagination it would take to conjure you up in one of my dreams."

TOM TAKES CHARGE

Tom had read about girls. He read about how they are each individually waiting to be swept off their feet. That they prefer a man who will take charge and maintain control of a situation. It lets them know that they're in capable hands, that they can trust him. And Tom knew that with trust came rewards greater than he could yet imagine.

Now he saw Lydia—perfect, gorgeous, Lydia with her shadowed eyes and perfume like liquid Sweet-Tarts. He saw her, finally standing by herself, a full court away from Kristie, and determined this would be his moment of glory.

He charged for her, making a bold line through the center of the dance, pushing himself through his inadequate peers who still believed the best way to express desire was by convulsing together in semi-circles of six or more.

Tom reached Lydia in full stride. His moment had come. Would Lydia know hers had come, too?

He planted his foot behind her heel, swiveled her into his arms, and as he strengthened himself to express his love for her, she fell through his grip and crashed straight onto the gymnasium floor.

THUNDERBIRD

Well, your grandfather, he was quite the Casanova when we were younger. I'll never forget the first time I slept with him. What? What do you mean you don't want to hear about this? You're old enough for it now. It's important you know these things. It'll lend you some confidence in your genes. How are you embarrassed? I don't understand. Everybody's bashful until the simple facts of life come to face. Let me simplify it for you. For you to exist, your father had to get your mother pregnant. And how did your mother come to exist? Because at twenty-four, I had the best breasts in the state and your grandfather couldn't keep his hands off them. But don't worry, since I've apparently "embarrassed" you, I'll spare you the rest of the details except to say that if your mother had come out a boy, his middle name would have been Thunderbird.

THE MOTIONS

Sometime during January he had begun the practice of kissing her goodbye as she slept every morning. Most mornings she did not budge, but occasionally her cheek would wrinkle into a smile and sometimes she would even muffle a goodbye herself.

In his mind, he knew he was going through the motions—him kissing her, him telling her he loved her every day. But he also believed that if he could continue to kiss her, continue to tell her that he loved her, perhaps one day it would also be true again.

And so he kept on. Through the winter, as the sun rose earlier and earlier into spring, and all through the hot summer: "Good morning, gorgeous. I love you," he repeated to her.

Until one stormy September morning, with the light seemingly still an hour too dim, he kissed her delicate cheek once more and stood ready to speak his scheduled phrase when she grasped his arm.

"I'm always asleep," she said. "I didn't want to miss it today."

Lowering himself towards her, he felt an awareness that had been missing from so many of his mornings. He saw the unnaturally small impression her head left on the pillow, the loose slip of hair clung to her lip, and of course her sleepy eyes that may or may not still have been dreaming as they gazed up towards him.

"Good morning, gorgeous," he whispered to her. "I love you." And he knew it to be true.

MISTLETOE

Mistletoe had been a total failure. They finally pulled the plug after a third woman believed the app represented a contractual obligation and chased her match seven blocks north on Park Avenue with an open can of pepper spray, threatening to use it on him if he would not kiss her. No, not even in the no-holds-barred world of GPS-location apps and niche dating services can you force two strangers to lock lips.

The signs had been long coming. Too many users had complained about the quality of their matches, or were too embarrassed when multiple times in a single day their would-be partners rejected them (An additional study showed users preferred a digital ignore to a face-to-face rejection—a fact the developers still contend, or would at least be too disappointed to believe.). There had also been other unfortunate incidents, like the married couple that had been pinged together, and more seriously, the poor woman who discovered a body in a garbage bin after a broken-hearted jumper left his cell phone on.

But as with any true failure, there is always at least one great success, and so the owners of SocialWow! Media were thrilled to receive the following letter, a full year after the app's demise:

"Dear makers of Mistletoe. Though I am sorry to hear your app shut down, I thought you would at least be excited to hear my story. Last December, as total strangers, I found my fiancée thanks to Mistletoe. We made out for two hours, freezing our asses off in broad daylight in the middle of Union Square. Six months later, he proposed to me. Thank you for changing my life. Sending a big kiss your way – Stacy Tuck."

THE LAST GIFT

"Now I have a surprise for you," speaks his Grandfather. "There is one last gift for you if you can tell me which present was my favorite this year."

The grandson begins to grin uncontrollably. He had in fact been disappointed when the steady train of presents ended but now the very mention of a single surprise gift takes hold of his imagination in a way that seems to dwarf the sleepless night before when the morning promised a tree full of them.

He considers long and hard, having difficulty even remembering what his Grandfather had received. A pair of pajamas, definitely. A funny sweater, he thinks, but that may have been for his Dad. And then it hits him, the giant golf club with the great big red bow resting against the fireplace.

"The golf club!" He shouts.

The Grandfather's eyes light up and he exclaims with his Grandson, "Yes! That's it! The golf club was my favorite! How did you know?" He asks.

"I don't know!" Responds the Grandson.

"Irregardless, you guessed correctly, your reward is due." The grandfather stands from the table, disappears for what feels like an eternity, and finally returns rolling a glossy black Schwinn.

The Grandson erupts. He runs through the house in circles no less than eleven times, each time, peeking again into the dining room to see if the black Schwinn is still there.

And so the tradition was born. Always, the Grandson's best gift saved for last. The Grandson merely had to guess which present had been his Grandfather's favorite. One year, a coffee maker; the next, tickets to a show.

Finally, on the Grandson's seventeenth Christmas, a year in which the Grandfather had received a Mediterranean cruise, the Grandfather asks his Grandson once more. "Which gift did I receive that was my favorite?"

And without hesitation, nor with any sign that could have preceded it—for this had been a happy year, not one of loss—the boy says, "I know the answer. Your favorite gift was us. It was having us all together."

"Very good," responds the Grandfather with tears welling as he reaches into his pocket. "And now you know a car is just a car."

BY THE PHONE

She had not called. It was nearing ten now but she had not called like she said she would.

He sat by the phone longer still. Thought back to how they had met earlier in the day. How he had helped her carry books into her shop.

Which was her favorite book? He asked. *The End of the Affair*, she replied. "A story has no beginning or end," he quickly recited and she had been impressed.

But he did not believe this himself. Stories do begin and they do end. Their story had begun today at the store and now he feared that tonight, because she had not called, their story would soon come to an end.

He was desperate to call her even though he knew he could not. Calling her would be a sign of panic. To panic would be to lose the girl. And he was not ready to lose her yet. No, he had not yet lost the girl.

He would stay by the phone and he would wait. Yes. He would wait.

I SEE YOU

I see you Meredith. I see you. It's 1958, our first night in our first home and you're racing from room to room. "It's your kitchen! It's your living room! All of it is yours!" I'm yelling...It's 2009, Thomas has just left with Kate and the grandchildren and you are crying because they have left so soon...Or 1963, when Thomas was born and you hemorrhaged. I couldn't see then, but I could, I could see the whole time, I knew you were going to make it. And you got so angry when you woke up and Thomas wasn't at your side. Mad at me for laughing, but I was just so thrilled to have you back...And our wedding night, August 2nd, 1957, when you put your dress back on in the middle of the night. You were so beautiful that day with your hair up, but I don't think you were ever so beautiful as that night. I see it all and I see you Meredith. I see you.

NEW YEAR

It's cold and you're far but I'm running my dear
My head was a mess but it's starting to clear
The revelers are out, they're spreading their cheer
But I can't celebrate until you are near

I remember last time we were sipping on beer
You and me on the couch with your new brassiere
A vision by the light of that plastic reindeer
And in my head, I said, "It's you I revere"

I'm thinking, maybe, we should start new careers
We could move to London, I'll be a Shakespeare
Then we'll fly to Cannes, catch a premiere
The house goes dark and then you appear

I'm almost there, I've just passed the pier
You know where we kissed the first night we were here
Maybe soon we can start sipping on beer
You and me on the couch with your new cashmere

No, I don't expect you to be sincere
And I haven't tried counting all of our tears
I just know if not now we'll soon disappear
And you're my only wish this year

JANUARY 1ST

There are streamers. There are bottles. There are
DVD's beside my face. *The Notebook. Home Alone. Mean
Girls.* The carpet is pink and I can feel my cheek pocked

with its imprint. To my left is an empty white couch. Why hadn't I slept on the empty white couch?

No one is here, though I do not know where here is. My keys are missing. I am also missing my pants and thus my phone. My pants have been replaced by gym shorts bearing the University of Maryland logo. I did not go to the University of Maryland.

Suddenly, a girl enters the room. She is wearing a University of Michigan t-shirt. I did attend the University of Michigan. She is wearing my t-shirt.

"Happy New Year," she says, staring at my carpet-pocked cheek.

"Happy New Year," I repeat.

"If…," she begins to say before stopping. She is pretty and there is something attractive about the quizzical look on her face.

"If I go out with you again," she continues, "can you promise not to throw up all over my comforter?"

REVERSE RESOLUTION

"Good news. I made a New Year's resolution."

"Oh yeah? What is it?"

"I decided I am *not* going to kiss you at least fifty times a day this year."

"How is that good news?"

"Because I've never kept a resolution."

HOT CHORES

"Hey, honey, you know what I find really sexy?"

"What's that?"

"When you do the dishes."

"Do you now? What else?"

"I think you look even sexier when you vacuum."

"You like that?"

"Oh yeah…"

"Well, you know what I think is sexy?"

"What? Tell me…"

"You know those heels you wear? To work? I like it when you take them out from the floor of the car."

"That is sexy. I'll do it. You want to watch?"

"Sure, and you know what else gets me in the mood?"

"What?"

"When I look down at the toothbrush holder and don't see any feminine products in it. It's like one of those you're-turned-on-by-what-you-can't-see kind of things."

"Right."

"Or, babe, you know what's really hot? In the shower, when you clean your hairballs. You know those brown things that might be alive? Pulsing like five dark-haired Cousin It's pasted to the glass? I'd really get excited to see you scrape those off."

"Okay, I get it. This isn't sexy anymore. I'll do the dishes."

"Don't worry, hot stuff, you're still number one with me. You might want to add this plate, though."

GAME SHOW

They met on a TV game show for love. She gained his respect by refusing his kiss until the end of the game. The surprise came when he set her example for the rest of the contestants.

At first she watched with a wry sense of humor as the other girls returned each night exasperated by their failures of seduction. Many of the girls were pretty, gorgeous even, and were left shell shocked when their best tricks—tickles, whispers, hands on laps, button slips, and at least one flat out assault—all came up empty.

Soon, however, her humor turned to admiration for the game's main player. He must have known, she considered, how absurd it was to find love as a pawn in a game show. But he tried anyways, and it seemed to her that the angrier the other girls got—some going so far as to question his sexuality on national TV—the more of a gentleman he became.

And so, one by one, the girls disappeared until there were none left but her.

It was not until she arrived for their final date, and saw him looking like a magazine cover in front of a crystal blue sea, that she realized she might even love him, too.

Which made what she was about to do all the more difficult.

"Now that you know it's you," he spoke, "and the game is over, will you finally kiss me?"

"No," she replied, aware of how much this likely hurt him. So she continued, "This entire game has been public. You falling for me has been public. And me falling more and more for you has been public. But I want our love to be private. They will always have this—our coming together.

But I want our first kiss to be ours and ours alone. I know I've asked a lot and I'm probably the last person that should have been allowed to play this game, but can you do that for me?"

"Yes," he said. "As long as you're with me, I've already won."

THE FORTUNE TELLER

One day, a fortune teller prophesized to a girl that she would soon meet a handsome man on a distant shore and that he would quickly become very important to her.

Three weeks later, as the girl traveled to Santa Monica, she met a boy who also lived in Cincinnati. By the end of the night he kissed her.

"How did you know?" The girl asked the fortune teller as soon as she returned home.

"What'll really knock your socks off is that you've seen him before. Sometimes we just have to be told to start looking."

FORBIDDEN LOVE

This had to be the last forbidden love, she thought. Class, race, ethnicity, religious background or sexual orientation. None of it mattered anymore. You could date a lesbian chimpanzee and hardly anyone but PETA would care.

But your boss? Not to say it hadn't been done before, but still, there was something edgy about it, almost electrifying. If it went well, it was bliss; poorly, and you'd be hit with a lawsuit faster than you could fix your hem line.

Okay, so maybe there were others. The stag Dad, the underage student, the sequestered juror—but she had to set limits somewhere. No messing with families and nothing downright illegal. At least not at the start.

Which left her boss: Dennis Pecker—forty-two, Divorced, N/K, saggy in the chest, favored brown, and successful in absolutely no category other than tenure.

In other words he was perfect. She'd already dropped looks as prerequisite to pleasure two years ago and my God did he have a big desk.

COCKTAIL NAPKINS

"Can you find love on a cocktail napkin?" He wrote.

"Yes," she said, taking the napkin and circling the word love. "But you'll have to look up to find a kiss."

THE BARBER

She was a barber. And she was hot.

Joe added up the number of times he'd been to Al's Barber Shop. Seven years multiplied by at least once a month. Eighty-four? And every time there was Al—grumpy, sardonic, Al. Always by himself despite the fact that the shop had two functioning seats:

"This one's for cuttin' and this one's for the meds to operate on in case I slip…"

But here was a second barber at last. And she was a knockout. Straight brown hair to her shoulder blades, a black tank top, and skin like olives plucked from a martini.

Where on Earth had Al found her?

"You're up," she said, impressing Joe with the way she'd assumed Al's matter-of-factness.

He jumped up and settled in for an experience that soon became otherworldly. At first, there was only the obvious: that when she worked up top her chest pressed into his shoulders; or when she cut around his ears, she peered in from mere inches away so that her breath landed hot on his neck.

But quickly Joe realized just how good she was, too. And fast. With the scissors, her hands were a blur. And God help him when she rubbed the warm lather on his neck and went to work with the straight blade. It was all he could do not to flinch.

By the time she finished, he was in love.

He came back the next week, and the next. On the third week, he nearly collapsed when Al called his name first.

"Not much to work on here, is there?" Al quipped.

"You know how I like our time together, Al."

"Sure you do," Al replied.

Joe peeked over to find the girl smiling. Al poked Joe with the clippers.

When the cut was finished, Al called Joe into the shop's back office for the first time ever.

He said, "Listen, Joe. That's my daughter you been staring at. Now I can't make her decisions for her, and I'm telling you, you give her trouble, and I'll cut you where it don't grow back. But go in there, ask her for her number, and you'll do okay...Oh, and Joe. I'm charging you double today."

GORDON LOVES BETTY

"Hey, Grandpa, how did you know you wanted to marry Grandma?"

"Because she said 'Yes.'"

"But that was after. How did you know you wanted to ask her in the first place?"

"You mean, how'd I decide to ask your grandma to marry me?"

"Yes!"

"Well, if I remember correctly, it was rainy that day. If it had been sunny, I was supposed to help a friend of mine build a fence. There wasn't much else to do, so I asked her to marry me."

"And did you tell her that you really really loved her?"

"You're full of questions, aren't you? Yes, if you must know, I told your grandma that I loved her."

"And that you wanted to spend the whole entire rest of your life with her?"

"I don't recall if that was part of it. I—"

"Wait, what am I about to miss?"

"Grandma! Grandpa's about to tell me about when he proposed to you!"

"Ha! I'd like to hear this."

"Well, as I was saying, I went over to your Grandma's house, I knocked on the door, and she opened it, and it was raining, so she asked me in, and I said, "Betty, I think I'd like to marry you. Would you like to marry me? And she said—"

"Wait, Gordon. That's not it at all. My God, you tell it like that and the poor girl will have nothing to look forward to. Penny, dear. You would have loved it. It was the most spectacularly sunny day, and Gordon here had come over, after asking my father for permission the day before, and he took me by the arm, out into the back, where we had an old tire swing he used to push me in. Well, right there had been our first kiss, and Gordon stopped beside it, and he asked if I would reach in, and I did, and out came the most beautiful diamond ring you've ever seen. And when I looked back, he was down on one knee, crying his eyes out, and he said, 'Betty, my beautiful, beautiful, Betty, I've always loved you, and if you'd let me, I'd like to keep on loving you so long as you live.'

"And, course I said yes."

"Awwww!"

"Swore it was raining."

"Gordon, you would've thought it was raining with all those tears coming out of your eyes!"

PRECIPICE

He stood in front of a great precipice. Before him he saw the answer to every question he had ever thought to ask. And more. In the precipice he began to see answers to questions that would not be asked for hundreds of years.

A pride began to swell in him unlike he had ever known. He remembered what Annie said, that he would be the next great discoverer. Galileo. Columbus. *Easton*.

Perhaps it was true. Perhaps they would one day learn that he had reached this place. But the pride he felt was for so much more than any recognition he sought. It was for all the others who had tried, for all those who had laid the groundwork, and for the one person who may have wanted this even more than he—Annie.

He peered further into the precipice, trying to make sense of the wonder before him: answers and questions raveling and unraveling, eons of life building and destroying itself within milliseconds. Amidst the chaos there seemed to be something neat taking place, something perfectly orchestrated and altogether unsurprising, like reading the last page of a book and understanding that this had been the only ending possible from the start.

And as soon as he began to understand all this, an isolated darkness filled his soul.

He swung his back to the precipice, searching impossibly for the red boosters of Annie's ship amongst the black of space.

She was gone. Annie was gone.

He tried to compose himself with the facts. That she'd been gone. For two years she'd been gone. That the mission had to be aborted and the only way either of them would ever know is if he were to enter the capsule alone.

"This is bigger than the both of us," they both agreed.

But it wasn't. It wasn't at all. Their calculation had been entirely wrong.

The message of his discovery would soon die with him—in a few months, or even a few seconds if he chose. There was no way to deliver it. It had died the moment he'd kissed Annie goodbye and the door to the capsule hissed closed.

And from Earth, the message would be the same. The stars would deliver it just as they had for billions of years.

Behind him, in colors he could not bear to watch, the forces beyond the precipice motioned on—an infinite supply of answers and not a one to fill the void in his heart.

He reached towards the expanse from which he had come. He reached towards Annie.

There was no way to contact her, but he prayed that a single mystery lay undiscovered still. That she would feel him reaching towards her and know that their love had been the only answer all along.

LUCKY NO. 42

"What are you grinning about?"

"I was thinking, I've been on forty-one first dates this year."

"And?"

"I just realized this will be my last one."

MY BABY'S BLUE

My baby's blue
Ohhh, my baby's blue
Because I said
Because of something that I said
Yes, I said something
Something I should not have said
And now she's sad
Ohhh, my baby's so very sad
Because when you say something that's very bad
That's when she'll get sad

And now my baby's blue
Ohhh, my baby's blue
Because I said, "I love you, I love you, I can't live without
    you, the ground starts to shake whenever I'm 'round
    you, you're heaven and stars, the queen of the cards,
    I'll always want to be wherever you are…"
But that's too far
Yes, I went too far
I said, "I love you"
And I went too far
Sometimes when you say those words
You gone too far
And I made her sad
So very sad
Because sometimes someone loves you, yes they do
But you can't love back
And when someone loves you
And you don't love back
Well then, that's when you get sad
And now my baby's blue
Cause she don't love me
The way I dooooooo

SEEK

She said, "Seek a love beyond what you can ever imagine: the kind that not only pulls you up when you're down and keeps you company when you're alone, but the kind that lifts you higher than the highest you've ever been and whose company you keep when the world won't leave you be. It exists. It absolutely exists. Believe in it. Find it. And when you do, show him the same kind in return—take him higher than he's ever been before and allow him to keep you when the whole world is his to keep."

IN TRIBUTE

In regards to the recent passing of Josephine Furling, I've been asked what it was like to know so intimately one of the twentieth century's great icons, or as one writer put long ago, and I on more than one occasion reminded her in jest, the woman who "Taught grace to be graceful." And indeed she was. So much so that you wondered if grace were the proper word at all, or if it were, why had it been used so loosely before now?

I did love Josephine, or Jo, as I called her (a small morsel I will offer to the media who will no doubt lick it up, thirstier than ever for the last remaining secrets of her life, thought for years to have been sucked dry of them). And while much has been written or made of our short romance between the years of 1967-1968, thankfully less was made of the friendship that followed. These of course being the years she met and fell in love with one of the richest spirits I have had the honor of knowing, Victor Towers (See, you will receive no anger or jealousy from me regarding this giant of a man), went on to raise three beautiful and gifted children, and offered the globe a behemoth of humanitarian work that many industrialized nations in tandem have yet to match. Yes, in the midst of solidifying her legend, she remained my friend—offering wisdom, humor, and support on many occasions when I might have gladly begged for a passing stranger's ear, let alone an unsolicited phone call re-routed from the Asian Pacific at the request of the world's most beloved woman.

And perhaps, wrongly or rightly, that is how I loved her. Not in the common lust for a Hollywood starlet, drunken by the circus that is its royal theater; and I'm afraid not in the intimate, between-the-sheets variety that serves as the basis of so many of our modern fairy tales; but in that gob smacked way that leaves me wondering how I could possibly have deserved the privilege of loving and being loved by the single greatest woman to have set foot on this Earth in the span of my lifetime.

CARL MEETS KEVIN

"What can I do for you?" Carl asked the flea-faced teenager shifting side to side on his doorstep.

"Uh, I'm here to pick up Angela," it spoke.

A sickness ran through Carl's belly.

"What's your name?"

"Kevin. Sir."

So this was Kevin. The object of Angela's teenage desires. Kevin, who appeared at Carl's home wearing girls' jeans, a graffitied t-shirt, and a fluorescent orange cap tilted forty-five degrees from center. Even the boy's failure of a beard had the quality of a hairy tarantula.

Carl's indigestion grew worse. He could hear Lynn's voice in his head, repeating, "Well, you were young once, too." To prove the point, she'd recently flashed an old yearbook photo of his she'd nicknamed Carl Travolta as a reminder.

But at least he had never dressed like a girl.

"What's that on your wrist," Carl asked the squirming boy.

"This? It's a love bracelet. Angela's got—"

Carl slammed the door shut. One day the women in his life would thank him.

THOMPSON QUIT TODAY

"Did you hear? Thompson quit today. He walked in at 7:30, scheduled a meeting with Rexford, and handed in his resignation. Apparently Rexford's real beat up about it, too. He freaking loved Thompson. He was always inviting him to his tailgates and stuff. Anyways, he told Lucy to cancel the rest of his morning meetings and hasn't been seen since.

"But that's just the half of it. Get this. When the meeting's over, Thompson had to have two H.R. reps follow him, right—watching him so he doesn't steal anything on the way out—so apparently he comes out of the office, walks a straight line to his desk and all he picks up is a pen and a single card from his stack. Literally, he leaves everything else behind: pictures, a calculator which Brent already hocked, his football...left it all.

"So he's got this pen and card in his hand, and H.R.'s looking at him like he's nuts, and all of a sudden, instead of turning towards the door, he beelines it the opposite way with both of the suits on his tail, all the way to, are you ready for this, to freaking Sophie Popple's desk."

"What's that? No, he'd never met her. Have you ever met her? Jeez, you stare at her enough all day, try saying hello once. But that's the point, right? Here he is, it's his last day, he's never had a chance to meet the girl since she got here, and the last thing he does before he walks out of here forever is go up to her, and he says, and I quote:

"'I'm quitting today and I would like to take you to dinner tonight, here, at nine,' and he writes down the name of the place on the card, hands it to her, and walks away."

"What'd she say? She didn't say a thing. She just stared at the card for the next thirty seconds before she turned around to find the suits pushing him out the door. I'll tell you, though, you've never seen a guy walk out of this place any happier than he did. He was on the freaking top."

SINCE BERMUDA

It's been three years. Three years since our last trip to Bermuda with me, Jules, Mom and Dad, and Liz. Liz, who kissed me on the grassy alter of the Unfinished Church, then again behind the rocks of Horseshoe Bay.

In retrospect, that was it. That was the top. If life is a series of peaks and troughs, Bermuda was Mt. Everest in the form of a pink sand beach. Nineteen years culminating perfectly so that everything that surrounded me was everything I wanted to be. A family, the girl I adored, and the chance to see at least one perfect sunset a year. That was my future and God did I love it.

But I guess if life were everything we ever dreamed of, it would be just that—a dream. And then there'd be no room for the waking up part, the ritual dawn which carries with it the hope of the day ahead; or the bedtime part, when in lying down at last, the darkness slowly reveals all that's been lost. The hours in between, those still moments when we ask ourselves why it's been three years since we last flew...

THEY WERE MUCH TOO QUICK

There's the story of the girl who skipped on the sun. She pranced and danced on beams of light that shed through her linen skirt but never burned her skin. She was much too quick.

And the story of the boy who ran across waves. He sought tsunamis to race and ran dry across oceans only to let his tired feet soak in lazy forest streams.

They met once. This girl of light and boy of water. They met where the dawn meets the tide and circled to find that place on the other side where the sea crests beneath the moon.

And for an instant, they allowed themselves to touch: their feet, which in motion had kissed no surface before, kissed off one another, hurtling them towards celestial bounds no others could reach…

ALL THE MANY REASONS

"So that's why you married me?"

"Well, among other reasons. I liked your intelligence, I saw how good you were with children, I knew I could trust you, and I had faith in where you were headed. You were also good with my parents, and brothers, and very considerate. I don't know, a whole bunch of reasons. Why? Why'd you marry me?"

"Because you always made me feel better than anyone else."

REPLAY

I wish there was a way to replay the moment we first met. We had class together, but I could not tell you when we first saw one another, or what our first words were. I wish I could tell you, but I can't. Did she smile, I hope, or did she float her eyes? Did she see through me from the start?

And what did I do? What would that perfect replay reveal? A slight tic, perhaps, unconscious to me then, a raised eyebrow to suggest that I had felt fate tap me on the shoulder, point to her and say, "That's her, that's the one. She's in charge of you now."

I wish I could go back. I'd like to go back. But if there's solace, it's the fact that she's beside me tonight. I'll tell her this, she'll roll her eyes again, and I'll be thankful for the present. Thankful our love replays still.

LEXINGTON AVENUE

Rush hour on Lexington Avenue. A workman's like rain drives the tourists' heads down and still they photograph the pavement. With each red light, he strides further north of the midtown crowds, further from his destination, hoping to find a single cab with a lit medallion.

One missed cab. Two. A third reads Off Duty, though the tourists never realize this, and a man in an LSU hat cusses all the same.

Already he is soaked through his suit. He would just as well toss his umbrella if it did not shield from the others that aim for his eyes.

On 60th Street, he strikes gold when a mother and three children exit beside him on the eastern corner. No doubt they are bound for Dylan's or Serendipity or both.

He holds the passenger door as they step out, conscious to appear gracious rather than desperate. When the mother says, "Thank you," he replies in kind and lunges himself into the vehicle.

As he shouts his instructions to the driver, and before he can shut the door, he hears a woman's voice appeal to him.

"I'm sorry," she says, "but are you headed near East 4th Street?"

He turns and sees her, petite and soaking in a black trench coat. No, not close at all, he thinks. Further still with the rain. But she is pretty and no doubt this is the type of Good Samaritan behavior he would also wish for.

"Hop in," he says.

"Thank you," she replies, repelling a sheet of water from her coat before closing the door.

While they ride, she plays with her phone and he counts streetlights. They pass no more than three consecutive green lights at a time. A half hour later, in the gridlock of the Village, three consecutive greens rotate before they clear a single one.

He peers at his fellow passenger for the first time. Her eyes are closed but her nose, small and pointed, twitches with sensations of its own. Further down, within her purse, her hands rest on a copy of *A Farewell to Arms*.

Was that with the bridge or with the nurse? Try as he might to recall, he cannot remember, and as he struggles to unlock an English class long forgotten, she wakes.

"Have you read it?" She asks.

"A long time ago."

"Are you much further?"

"No, not so far," he says, knowing it would take another half-hour to circle back and west.

"Then take this as a gift along with my fare," she says, handing him the book with a ten dollar bill atop. "Perhaps one day you can read it to me."

She opens her door to a newly calmed drizzle.

"But how will I be able to reach you?"

"Check the bookmark," she says, shutting the door and racing away with her bag above her head.

He opens to where the bookmark lay and reads from the top of the page. So it is the nurse story, he thinks. He lifts the bookmark, in this case, simply a business card:

Emily Lorrie, Vice President, Sales, Cunning Books.

SIMPLE PLEASURES

He served her ice cream in a mini baseball helmet with whipped cream and a cherry on top. Little did he know that this exact presentation had been one of her favorite recurring childhood memories—Sunday evening dinners with her parents at The Ground Round, capped always with an ice cream sundae served in a tiny collectible helmet.

No, he could not have known this, or the effect it would have on her, that in this moment she would at long last fall in love with him. But perhaps that is for the best. So frequently we think of love as a complicated thing when more often it has simpler pleasures in mind. In this case: a treat, a trinket, and the trusted company of another.

LOVELY LUCETTA

Lovely Lucetta
From the day that I met you
You've had the better of me
You're a chronic bed wetter

Have a wicked bad temper
And all those crazy sexual needs
But tempt me Lucetta
I'll never forget you
Cause you've got the better of me
Once I moved to your city
You stood up and quit me
Said my future's as bright as a cave
So I moved away quickly
Ten months later you found me
"Just Married" in East L.A.
You slapped me in the face
Called me a disgrace
And said, "Make love to me like I was your maid."
No, I don't get you Lucetta
You change like the weather
Sun today, tomorrow a hurricane
You're a Category 5
The queen of the hive
And you've got the better of me
One day I think I'll be free
Of you and your misery
The 4 A.M. calls, the chain and the balls
Your collection of antique cutlery
But then I'm reminded
Of the day that you minded
When I went for a walk by the falls
You said "If you leave me again
You'll wish you had fins
So don't go walking alone"
Oh Lovely Lucetta
From the day that I met you
You've had the better of me
Your grace is unmatched
You're an angel with sass
And you've got the better of me

WINDOW

A strange thought occurred to me just then: This is what it's like to love as an adult. My love had grown up. The adoration was still there, that would never leave, but something new, something different—a little bit inspiring, and even a little bit warm and fuzzy, like something glowing inside of me because of her.

In a word, admiration. I saw her dreams and knew they had become my dreams. Her wishes, my wishes. I wanted them to come true, every last one of them. I wanted her to believe how well she could make this world, because for the first time, I was seeing it as she saw it. And it was a better world. So much better than the one I knew.

DIG DEEPER

"You said you love her, yes?"

"Yes."

"Dig deeper. The word love is what we say when we haven't bothered to feel anything else. Do you miss her?"

"Absolutely."

"How then? How do you miss her? Like a puppy who sits by the front door all afternoon waiting for its owner or like a shipped soldier misses his girl back home and feels her like the one phantom limb he can't touch."

"Like the soldier, I guess?"

"So you're comparing yourself to a Veteran are you? Besides being plagiaristic, it's insulting. Remember this, your passion for this girl is unique. No one on Earth will ever experience it exactly as you have. Now start again, what makes what you feel for this woman totally unique?"

"I…"

"I once spent five months cleaning my wife's bottom of her own feces. Due to the circumstances of the time, that was unique. Have you done nothing for this woman? If so, you had better run home to her before you find her gone. Beg her for forgiveness when you get there: for your lack of devotion, your lack of courage when it comes to fulfilling the needs and desires of her life. How about that? Can you at least say what it is *you* desire? If not that, then there is no hope. None at all. So what is it? What of her do you desire?"

"Everything. I want everything that she is."

"That's it! Now you're starting to learn."

NEON STARS

I miss our lake days, cooling our feet beneath the dock and waiting for the fireworks to ignite the other side. Do you remember how they mirrored each other, the surface and the sky? I miss our winter nights, blood rushing through our frozen skin and not minding that the sheets felt like fire to touch. The board games and wine and did my cheeks redden much? I miss our road days, the longest days, chasing the sun as far as we could. Curbside beneath neon stars, three beers each, and wishing that we would. I miss the days that haven't come to be, and the night that's over soon. I miss what I haven't lived yet, missing these heavenly days with you.

LEGEND

"There is a phrase which suggests that anybody can do a great thing once, but to do a great thing over and over, day after day, that is the surest sign of a legend.

"In love, my dear, you are a legend."

SNOW ANGELS

I trailed her down the center of County Road, one foot in front of the other, trudging within tire marks as the lampposts gave form to the snow globe around us.

Every twenty steps or so, she would stop, turn, and say, "I can't go any further. I need another kiss."

I would kiss her, she would smile, kiss me once more to be sure, and continue on her way, twenty more steps to cover before "needing" to kiss again.

Nearly halfway through our mile long trek, she dipped to the ground and began to swing her arms and legs.

"What are you doing?" I asked.

"Making snow angels," of course.

It had been a rhetorical question, a reflex to myself, but there was no use in correcting her. She had seen the actual answer on my face. What else would she be doing besides making snow angels at this silent hour?

What else but stealing my heart.

START UP

He thought back to a year ago, when they met at a bar and within two hours she had nearly convinced him to quit his job and open an online art gallery with her.

"I'll have to think about it," he said at last, always the more cautious one.

"Okay," she said. "Call me tomorrow when you're a little more sober and you can decide then. Just to warn you, though, you're going to say yes."

He laughed at this, said he hoped she was right, and wished her a good night.

Five sleepless hours later, he called her.

"I told you you would say yes," she said.

"One question first," he said.

"What's that?"

"Why me?" He asked. "We just met. Why do you think I'm the right person to go in on this with?"

"Because you won't let me fail," she said, so matter-of-factly that even a year later he wondered how she could possibly have known.

"Okay," he replied. "Let's do it."

The next day they met and outlined a business plan. He would develop the site, she would attract the local talent. On Monday, they each handed in their two-week notices and that evening celebrated their launch over a half-pepperoni pie from Papa John's.

From then on, the events of the year were a blur: going live in March with only a few of her paintings to display, their first sale to a non-relative four nervous weeks later, breaking even for the first time on September 5th, the mention in *Avec Belle* in October which doubled their sales overnight, and hitting a million dollars in revenue in

December. All of it, the whirlwind dream they'd always read about.

Then he thought of her. How'd she'd gone from stranger to partner overnight, and during Thanksgiving, how after a long and heated discussion on the dangers of mixing business with pleasure, she became his lover. How thrilling it had been to finally admit that to one another after such a long period of inhibition. How perfect their story had been.

"Do you remember what you said to me a year ago?" He asks her now, as they celebrate the one year anniversary of their partnership with a half-pepperoni pie.

"What's that?"

"You said I wouldn't let you fail. And I don't know how you could have come up with that, or known it to be true, but what I wanted to say in return is, thank you. For believing in me, too. I could never have done any of this—I could never have quit, and could never have succeeded the way we have—if not for the fact you wouldn't let me fail either."

THE ENDLESS SEASON

It was the type of February day that if he allowed himself to block out the chill, and fall into the sweet blue sky, he might also convince himself that it were June and in a moment she would round the corner in a linen yellow dress with white flip flops flapping beneath. Instead, she appeared wearing one of those Eskimo length parkas with a puffy hood bundled over her head. The chill did not return to him, however. Inside, the warmth remained. His girl had rounded the corner, with a smile on her face, and in his heart, at least, he knew the seasons did not change.

VALENTINES

Molly felt like she was going to cry. Her Mom had said that if she gave everyone in the class a valentine, then they wouldn't believe a word Annabelle said. And, she added, they would like Molly just as much, if not even more than her.

So Molly had given every classmate a Reese's Pieces valentine, her absolute favorite candy, but so far, no one had given her a valentine in return.

Not even Hailey, not even Beth, and not even Miles whose valentine she wanted most of all.

Directly across from Molly, Annabelle sat stacking her valentines. "See," she whispered once Mrs. Hawthorn turned away, "nobody likes you."

It was the worst Molly had ever felt in her whole life. She felt so small, practically invisible, and she had to scrunch the back of her eyes as hard as she could to keep her tears from pouring out.

Don't cry, she thought, over and over, even though all she wanted to do, more than anything, was cry.

"Very good class," announced Mrs. Hawthorn. "Last but not least, the Red table. Go ahead Red table."

Bobby, Raj, Eileen, and Peter all circled the room with their bags of valentines. They reached Molly's Yellow table in order, and in the same order they each gazed nervously between Annabelle and Molly before handing the last of their cards and candies to Annabelle.

Molly dug her face into her arms and gave up on not crying. She didn't care if she left an ocean of tears on her desk. Valentine's Day was over and she hadn't received a single valentine. Now she even hoped they would all see it, see her crying just so they would know how bad they had made her feel.

As she pressed her face as hard as she possibly could into the nook of her elbow, she felt a tap on her shoulder.

"What?" She muffled, keeping her head down, hoping it wasn't Mrs. Hawthorn.

"Molly," a boy's voice spoke.

She lifted her head and wiped across her face with her forearm. Miles was standing beside her with a red box held out. The box had her name on it.

"I'm sorry I took so long," he said, opening the box to reveal the dozens of valentines he had received from every member of the class, "but I wanted to wait until I had enough for you. Will you be my valentine, Molly Roland?"

THE DARING PLAN OF BENJAMIN WOOD

This is the story of how Benjamin Wood, twenty-five years old, born, raised, and employed as an engineer of baby shampoo formula in Cincinnati, Ohio, developed the daring plan to have Courtney Wexford, twenty-six, born, raised, and employed as a Multi-Platinum recording artist in London, England, fall desperately in love him. It also happens to be the story of how it came true.

GRAVESTONES

George F. Hackett
March 2, 1922 – April 14, 1995
Free at last…

Melinda Graves Hackett
June 15, 1923 – January 30, 1997
Hope you enjoyed your vacation, George

TELEGRAPH

GB NQ065 PARIS 22 15TH
NLT DESJARDINS
     NEW YORK
ARRIVED WELL STOP HIGGINS SICK STOP ADDING
LONDON STAY THREE DAYS STOP ROYALS REQUEST
STOP FRENCH GIRLS VERY PRETTY STOP DO NOT
WORRY STOP THEY ENVY YOUR BEAUTY STOP
BACK FOR YOUR BIRTHDAY STOP THEN WE MARRY
STOP KISSES OVER THE ATLANTIC

GEORGE

23 EAST 60TH ST

INTERVIEW WITH ALAN FIELD – PART 1

WILL WEEKS: Now, here you are, you're forty years in, still going strong. Some have called you Rock and Roll's greatest love song writer of all time. You've had twenty-three singles reach multi-platinum. And on the other hand, some have questioned your own love life, having been through four marriages now, and whether that should still make you an expert. So which is it? Do you still believe in love?

ALAN FIELD: Do I still believe in love? Well, that's sort of like saying do I still believe in gravity? Do I still believe in the one thing that's managed to keep me attached to the Earth all this time? Or perhaps it's the opposite. Perhaps it's been gravity holding me down while love was the opposite force. Love kept wanting me to float away and I've been fortunate to have my good friend gravity holding me steady…

But yes, sort of a backwards way of saying, yes. Absolutely I believe in love.

You mentioned the success I've had. If you're asking for proof, that love exists, I think you have it in those figures. You don't sell millions of albums by preaching something that doesn't work. You give them something they believe in. Whether or not I've done a good job of telling it is for someone else, but that's still thirty-two million people believing in love, hearing a song, or a lyric, somehow relating it to their own life and saying, "Yea, I know what that feels like. Feels pretty good, doesn't it?"

And if you're asking me personally, even after four marriages, if I still believe in love, the answer there is yes, as well. I still love all four of them, for example, all in different ways, I suppose.

In the grander scheme, though, I think what we have in this life is very special. We all know that, but we don't always think about it. So multiply this idea with the odds of meeting someone who can really put this idea in context for you—who really makes you say, "Wow, this is more special than I even imagined."

At that point, love begins to transcend, am I right? I don't care what religion you are, if you're able to share that with someone, even for a short period of time, there's something very spiritual happening there. Something that makes you really happy to be alive.

And I guess that's the whole point, isn't it? Love makes you happy to be alive.

INTERVIEW WITH ALAN FIELD – PART 2

ALAN FIELD: It was interesting working on Love Drug because I had just split with Marilyn, that was wife number two if you're keeping count, and I was feeling really down on myself and using all sorts of things at the time because that was popular at the time.

WILL WEEKS: Drugs. You were using drugs, right?

ALAN FIELD: Yes, drugs. Very creative of me, right? *Love Drugs*. Spent a lot of time on that one, didn't I? Though actually, the album came about because I literally woke one morning in Henry's birdcage—Henry toured with a cock-atoo that year—and I'd woken up having soiled myself in this birdcage. Now more worrisome to me was I couldn't remember how I'd gotten there, but I knew it had some-thing to do with this breakup. That really stuck with me, this concept that love can hit you like a drug. It can enter your bloodstream and get you just as high as a mad hatter, only to, at the very end, leave you a total wreck. Literally, waking in a birdcage waiting for the next hit.

Needless to say, in retrospect, it was just a terrible concept. What was worse probably was becoming famous for such a bad concept. Just a terrible lesson for a twenty-six year old. So much success on something so awful. That's how you release *Liquid Bedroom* six months afterwards.

WILL WEEKS: So your opinions have changed?

ALAN FIELD: Oh yes. I mean I suppose love can exist like that. But it's just a terribly selfish and destructive way to love.

WILL WEEKS: In other words, don't do that.

ALAN FIELD: Ha, yes. Don't do that. That's how you get a third ex-wife. Believing things like that might work.

You know, the funny thing is that people still come up and say how happy that album makes them feel. I hope I hav-en't just ruined it for them, telling them how the inspiration was me waking up in a birdcage filled with my own feces.

INTERVIEW WITH ALAN FIELD – PART 3

WILL WEEKS: Last question. So many people have listened to your music through the years. The songs have become a part of their lives in many ways. After forty years, do you think you could piece it all together? How, according to Alan Field, perhaps the greatest living songwriter of all time, should people love in their own life?

ALAN FIELD: Well, we all love in our own ways, don't we? That's what makes us unique. That's what makes the different loves we share unique. But if I were to try to summarize what it's all been about. Hmm. That's quite difficult…

Love with all you've got. That's it.

When you're on stage, you have to give it your all, right? You have to really let it go so that the fan in the very last chair in the very last row of the arena feels it just the same as someone who's standing up front? Love like that. With everything you've got. It doesn't always work—some nights you just don't have it like you had it the night before—but no matter what, I promise you, if you give it all you've got, they'll be shaking in the balconies well after it's over.

So that's it. Give it all you've got. Make her shake.

How's that for a Rock and Roll answer?

END OF TRANSCRIPT

CANDLELIGHT

Twenty seven feels like twenty three next morning and you were there with fresh sheets totally complete your world in your hands and your world stepped sideways and twenty five was twenty six all the time apart all the candles in the dark new loves new gloves old feelings old feelings of you in the park wrap a circle round the pond beyond the distance I went for you go there go there again through the castle down the avenue cross the west side to the small city and iron lights where you and I can dance by the small candle light just you me and our candlelight

LAST KISS

This would be their last kiss. He knew it instinctively, felt it in her lost grip, heard it in her last words: "I'm ready," she had spoken two hours earlier and he knew it be true. Her heart rate had slowed and at times her eyelids would close for intervals long enough he feared they might never open again. When they did, she gazed at him with pupils dilated so wide it was as if she were standing at the far end of a long tunnel where no light could reach.

No, he was not ready. Could not be ready. But he also knew it was not his choice. The days of his willing her to live had long passed. So he bent down, matched his lips to hers and felt the warmth which had not yet vanished, searched for a faint pulse beneath the thin white coat of dried saliva. When he opened his eyes, she was looking towards him and it was as if a flare had sparked from within those tunneled depths. For a brief moment her frosted irises melted into their familiar sea blue and she was there, completely aware.

"There you go," she seemed to say. "Now you're ready."

And he knew it to be true. That he'd given her the last gift this Earth would supply her, and she to him, the greatest gift Earth ever would supply.

LET'S GO

He thinks this might be the happiest moment of his life. So often the past, present, and future trouble to align with one another: a past we're not entirely proud of, a present that wishes to be someplace else, or a future which has trouble anticipating. For him, though, they seemed to have each lined together in storybook fashion: last night he married the girl he'd spent his life dreaming of, today he watches her pack (Forgivably slower as she stops often to admire her new jewel), and where they are headed seems particularly gift wrapped, a surprise that is sure to dull even the brightest revelations of the past.

"Are you ready?" She asks at last.

Ready? He thinks. Ready to be your husband. Ready to love you, to idolize you, to care for you, and receive all that you will give in return. Ready to share this beautiful life with you.

Absolutely, he is ready.

"Let's go."

STILL LIFE

They say
Take a still life
That I could still
Have your life
A moment
Caught for all of
Time
And focus
On the green grass
Your white dress
In motion
Emotions
Out of focus
The sun sets
I'm hopeless
Love
Your reach
Beauty
And the trees
May you out run
The shadows
As far as you please
They say
Take a still life
That I could still
Have your life
A moment
Caught for all of
Time

A GOOD FRIEND

"There's only one solution," George said to his inconsolable friend.

"What is it?" Peter asked.

"I'm going to get you drunk. Obscenely drunk."

"Think it will help?"

"Peter," George said, "you have a sickness. And it's buried deep inside you. If you'd like, you could go see a doctor, spend thousands of dollars to repeat some mantra about not needing Alice to love yourself, or, you can spend one horrific night with me, your best friend, and we'll try to get to the bottom of this together. So, no, I cannot promise you it will help, but if you feel like you need to touch rock bottom, I'll get you there faster than anyone else."

"Okay, then. Let's do it."

And drunk they did get. Terrifyingly drunk. More drunk than Peter had ever been before.

Still, George was not satisfied. With each drink Peter's sickness only grew worse. At 10 P.M., he wailed "You're not Alice!" at the table beside theirs. An hour later, he ripped open a salt packet and cryptically spelled with his finger, "*A Dover Blue.*"

At midnight, George decided to test him.

"Do you think you can win her back?" George asked.

"Maybe?" Peter gurgled.

"Not drunk enough," George answered, racing to the bar for another round.

By two A.M., George sensed he was close. Returning from the bathroom, he found Peter crouched like a fetus in a booth, sucking the thumb of a girl who wore a "*Save the Jellyfish*" t-shirt two sizes too small and was herself sucking on a Heinz ketchup bottle with her free hand.

"Do you think you can win her back?" George asked again, removing the thumb from Peter's mouth.

"Strawberries," Peter said.

Ecstatic, George yanked Peter up and rounded him over his shoulder.

"We may have done it!" He shouted.

"Strawberries," Peter repeated. "Alice loved strawberries."

George dropped Peter to the floor. He thought about what it would mean to go any further. Past the stages where noise, and flesh, and light ignite the senses; beyond where dizziness seeks balance and retching relays relief. The goal was to cure Peter, not kill him.

As George looked up, with his legs straddling his helpless friend, he found his answer sitting across the bar: a magnificent blonde who seemed at this precise moment to be the antithesis of the hell they had tried so hard to breach. Yes, a guardian angel who might just save them both…

The next afternoon, Peter entered the kitchen, looking as if the Grim Reaper had deemed him unfit to enter the netherworld, and flopped beside George.

"It didn't work," he said. "I still miss her."

"I know," Peter responded.

"What good was it then?"

"For you? None whatsoever. You have the liver of the gods. The only thing that will cure you is time. But on the bright side, I looked like an absolute hero to this blonde chick last night when I carried my sobbing and drooling best friend-with-a-broken-heart out of the bar."

MRS. TALISMAN'S GARDEN

When I was young, we had this neighbor, Mrs. Talisman. Her husband had died before I was even born and she lived alone in the house next to us. She never had children, but she was always very nice to us, and every day we'd see her tending to the small garden she had. Sometimes I would even go over and help and she'd teach me different tricks like how spreading tea leaves will give the plants more nutrients.

One day a delivery man came and must have taken a liking to her, because the next day he arrived with a fresh set of chrysanthemums. I remember watching from across the way, he had no idea what he was doing, but she walked him over to the garden and showed him how he could properly plant his chrysanthemums.

Five or six days later he came back with another small pot, this time tulips, and she helped him to plant them once again. This went on all summer, every few days he would arrive with a new set of flowers, and together they would add to the plot she had made for him beside her mailbox. By the end of the summer they had made this beautiful garden together.

Well, I always thought that was the most romantic thing I'd ever seen. And ever since then, I guess it's what I've been hoping to find. Someone else who sees something beautiful in this world, too. Someone else who I can build my own type of garden with.

TED AND SUE

You haven't heard of Ted and Sue, but you will. You haven't seen their faces on billboards or on the covers of magazine racks yet, but you will. Or together on *The Today Show*, strutting down the red carpet in L.A., or of their new partnership with Jay-Z and Taylor Swift, but you will. You might not know their histories now: how this starlit couple met in a record store in Brooklyn, how they started a band and created their first film together using only their cell phones, but you will. Years from now you'll still be reciting your favorite lines from that movie, and you'll remember the speech they gave at the Oscars of how the only way dreams come true is if you have the faith in yourself to go after them—the faith to sing if you're a singer, the faith to film if you're a filmmaker, or the faith to write if you're a record keeper of the world as you imagine it, as you wish it would be.

No, you don't know Ted or Sue. Not yet. But you will.

WONDER

It starts with wonder. How nothing became something, and how something could be as beautiful as this. Planets spinning around the sun, the moon tugging at the seas. Four seasons, spring I know best, but even winter offers the perfect shade of white. See miracles abound: see life, even death. See chaos orchestrating; believe it might also be a plan. To be conscious, to be aware; to know how special this really is. I marvel at all the wonder. And then the day ends and you return home. Wonder of wonders, nothing so wonderful as you.

WHO ARE THESE KIDS?

"Do you ever wonder if maybe our children were switched at birth and that somewhere, instead of the aliens we have, there are two perfectly normal children sleeping quietly right now?"

"Sure, babe…"

"Do you think that means we still have to take care of them? Maybe there's a shoemaker or someone that can take them as indentured servants."

"I'm sure there is…"

"Tommy would make a great cobbler. He's good with hammers. Did you see what he did to my side view mirror?"

"Yes, I did…"

"I don't know about Billy. What's a good job for someone who likes to spit on everything? Maybe he can shine the shoes after Tommy puts them together. You know they don't even look like us. I can't even accuse you of cheating because they're like your opposite. You're short, they'll be tall. You're quiet, they're loud. You're civilized, they're demonic."

"They're not demonic…"

"Close. You saw Bobby try to bite the Packard's dog. The dog didn't have rabies. Bobby did."

"Can I go to sleep now?"

"Almost. Let me ask you something. Do you really love those boys?"

"Yes. And you do, too."

"I know. That's the hard part."

FERRY

He noticed that she always rode on the deck of the ferry when she could. Even during the winter, when every other passenger huddled within the heated hull, she would brave the elements alone.

For months and months he watched until one not-too-cold March morning, he approached her, feeling the urge to ask her why.

"I don't know," she said. "Mostly it's because I just like to be outside, especially when I'm about to spend the next ten hours inside. And I always loved the water. That could be it. Maybe something else, too."

"What's the something else?"

"Would you have noticed me if I had been in there all this time, reading a magazine or the paper every morning? Just like the rest?" She asked.

"Probably."

"Probably. Possibly. You never know. Well, I always had this feeling, if I were the one to stand out here, all by myself, maybe one day some handsome man who wouldn't mind a little chill would come and talk to me...Did it work, you think?"

"Well, I don't know anything about being handsome, but..."

"Don't worry," she stopped him. "I think it worked."

TUGBOAT

"Is he loaded?"

"Nah, man, I've seen his place. Total dump. Lives with two roommates. Rides a bike to work."

"He's not some tech wizard, is he? Starting a company in his basement that's going to be worth like a billion dollars?"

"Nope. Accountant."

"What are we missing? I bet you he's got a hash farm. Like *Weeds* or something."

"Did you know he doesn't even drink?"

"Well what else could it be? She's freaking perfect to look at and he looks like a walrus with syphilis."

"Dude, you're not telling me anything I don't already know."

"Wait, Vickie will tell me. Yo Vickie, got a question for you."

"Yeah? What's that?"

"You see Tugboat over there? How on Earth did he land Jane?"

"You serious?"

"Yeah."

"You guys are such tools. You really want to know?"

"Yes."

"'Cause he was the only one of you pricks to have the stones to go and talk to her."

BAD COMIC

Love makes us do funny things. Like yesterday, I drove to work without putting my pants on. Actually, that was because I mixed three Percocets with a Ten Hour Energy, but still, love makes you do funny things. I tried to do something funny once, but I guess love didn't have a sense of humor that day because I ended up married. People are always saying love is blind. So you know what I did? I wrote down the type of girl I'm looking for and then I figured out how to write it again in Braille. Just in case I meet love. Isn't that fun to imagine love as some random person walking down the street who can make all your wishes come true? You can just be like, "Hey, Love!" and love will shout back, "Hey buddy, have I got a winner for you today!" But then you start to imagine other emotions and it's not so good. "Hey Angry!" and then you get punched in the face. Or, "Hey, Bored!" and bored says back, "..." You know the song, I Would Do Anything For Love? My ex-girlfriend gave me a lists of all her "That's." Watch baseball, eat at Subway, move to Cleveland. And I'm like, we don't even live in Cleveland. And she's like, exactly. So the last "That" she wrote was she wouldn't watch *Shawshank* with me again. So then I made my own list, I wrote one word. I wrote, "You." That's why she's my ex-girlfriend now. My current girlfriend came up with the idea of naming our apartment Love. That way we can say that whenever we're home we're "In Love." But I think the other reason she does it is so that every time she goes out with her friends at night she can safely say that she's "Out of Love." Needless to say, I like Love, so I try to stay home a lot. Though sometimes I worry that means half the time I'm just in Love with myself.

BEFORE SLEEP

I met someone tonight. Her name is Mary Beth. She teaches in Summit. She moved here a year ago from North Carolina and lives in Chatham. And, yes, since I know you'd want to know, she is pretty.

I met her just like you said I should. I signed up on one of those websites, and put up a couple pictures of myself and tried to describe myself which was pretty hard. You would laugh if you read it. "Hi, my name is Kevin. I work in pharmaceuticals. I like tennis and movies." I don't know how it works or what you're supposed to say. It's very strange. Maybe it's because we met in person first, but I feel like with you it had been so natural, it was never a checklist, we just clicked. Just like that, I had my new best friend and it was like I knew everything about you and really nothing at all at once. That's what made it exciting…

I do think the date went well. We agreed to meet again. I told her I would take her to La Campagne on Thursday. Don't worry, I won't suggest Mayfair's.

I just want you to know I'm trying I guess. I don't know if you're sitting up there happy for me, or maybe even a little bitter, hearing this, I know I would be, but I'm trying. And it's hard, because I don't know what I'm doing, or if it's supposed to be serious or not serious, and I don't want to lead her on if I'm not ready even though I have to try, even if it feels like cheating. I know it's not, but that's what it feels like. Especially if I believe you're up there like I do, and I always want you to know that I love you, so much, and you're still my best friend and the only girl I've ever loved…

I love you Gwen. I guess that's what I really wanted to say tonight, that I'm trying to be happy like you said, but I can't do that without telling you I love you.

NO MORE SAD SONGS

"Why do you write so many sad songs?" She asked.

"I don't know," he said. "I suppose they tend to carry more weight."

"Well, what about me? You fell in love with me, right?"

"Yes."

"And when you did, you were happy about it, right?"

"Yes."

"And didn't it feel like the world had been lifted off your shoulders? Like you could go out and achieve anything because you had me supporting you no matter what?"

"Yes."

"Perfect. Now go and write me a happy song."

THEN I MET YOU

I wanted to be an actor
Then I met you
They gave me Best Picture, Director, too

I wanted to be a pitcher
Then I met you
I threw a no-hitter, in Game 2

I wanted to be a writer
Then I met you
My bestselling follow up is coming soon

I wanted to be a painter
Then I met you
We'll catch my exhibition at the Louvre

I wanted to be a rock star
Then I met you
Got myself a new gig, opened by U2

I wanted to be a lover
Then I met you
And now all my dreams have come true

ANDY LOVES AMERICA

Andy had gone to find love in America. He even made a website, AndyLovesAmerica.com, to track his aimless route in search of the girl of his dreams. Within a week, and before he could escape the borders of Virginia, he received over 1,800 requests for dates stretching from Portland, Maine, to Portland, Oregon. Using the dates as guideposts, he traveled from one town to the next honoring as many as he could (He maxed himself out in Charlotte with seventeen one-on-one's in a single exhausting day that included stops at three separate Checkers. Two weeks later, he wised up and arranged a single speed dating session in a mini-mall near Chattanooga). But as the weeks and dates ran on, he began to wonder if he had placed himself in a vicious trap. He had met nine Whitney's already, but in truth, had he really met a single one at all? And so, while stopped at a gas station named Joe's in Clarksville, TN, beneath the southern border of Kentucky, which hovered like a giant estrogen filled chicken wing on his map, he decided he needed to bring the expedition back to its roots. He needed to go off the grid in America. He would keep traveling, but this time his future love-to-be would not see him coming, could not prc-arrange for him to attend her nephew's Christening or sign him up in advance for bull riding school. When he ultimately found her, it would be because his road of destiny had finally converged with hers—just the way love ought to be in America.

HALFWAY

"I think I'm going to take a break now," he said at last.

"But why? I loved reading your stories."

"And I loved writing them for you."

"Then why do you have to stop?"

"There's always another story to write, but there's one that's more important than the rest."

"Which one is that?"

"Our love story. That's the story I want to work on next."

SPRING

THE TREE HOUSE

He built her a tree house.

"But why?" She asked.

"Climb up, you'll see."

So she climbed into the blue colonial tree house with the white shudders where inside he'd created a studio. Several of her paintings hung on the walls and in the corner, beside an open square window overlooking the valley, a fresh canvas sat on an easel awaiting its transformation.

It was a studio in the trees, the studio of her childhood dreams.

"This is too much," she said.

"We could tear it down."

"No! I mean…"

"You mean no one's ever given you a gift like this and you don't know what you could give in return."

"Yes."

"Hopefully that means I'm getting closer. I remember feeling the same way the day you married me."

TWO MILLION

Dear Gorgeous,

I am writing this, quite simply, because I know it will be read over two million times. And because I know how special it will make you feel knowing two million people read a love letter addressed to you.

Xoxo

GOODBYE HOUSE

He ran over directions one last time with the movers. "That's right, Memphis, Tennessee. We'll be there waiting for you." As the truck turned out of the driveway, he re-entered the house for what would be the last time.

How bare it looked now, stripped of furniture, with rugs pulled up, and walls naked without pictures. The sound of his steps echoed from one room to the next.

He found the off-white spot he had tried to hide— his first plaster repair after Jimmy had gotten hold of a hammer, and for no reason in particular, chose to perform demolition.

Upstairs, the kids' bathtub where he spent an hour nearly every night, bathing Jimmy at first, then he and Lucy together, until it was Lucy all by herself.

The bedroom. Even though it had been trucked away, the bed still seemed to take up space, as if he could close his eyes, take the three and a half steps towards it and fall sideways beside Olivia.

They would sleep together in the hotel tonight, but he began to wish they could spend one more night alone in this room.

In the master bath, he washed his face clean, dried it with his sweat stained t-shirt, and thought how foolish it was to get emotional over a house. He doubted whether a funeral had ever caused him to cry before.

But cry he did. Because as silly as it seemed, he did love this house. Loved it very much. And how could he not? For this house had loved his family so very well, too.

COWORKERS

They met in one of those hypersensitive periods of her life, following the accidental death of her grade school friend, Anna Kroger, who died instantly when a gutter dislodged, sending a sheet of ice flying two stories down and through the window beside which Anna had been taking her bar exam. She had not spoken to Anna in nearly three years, but as when death occurs, time is a relative. Three years may have been three days and now Anna was one less friend to share on this Earth.

He was her coworker, newly arrived from a rival firm and eager to put in long hours to get ahead. Charged with bringing him up to speed while simultaneously discouraged by the thought of spending the majority of her twenty-sixth year confined to a desk terminal, she chose to hold many of her mentoring sessions at McCullough's, the local watering hole known best for its pickle-backed shots.

Naturally, focus on ad space and spending plans quickly drifted into the philosophical, the therapeutic, and, in not so long a period of time, the flirtatious.

Ground rules were promptly laid. First, no one in the office must ever know. Second, their arrangement did not fall under friends with benefits. They were not friends and whether any real benefit was occurring was speculative at best. This was not, in her words, a joy ride.

As it turned out, she was also pleased to learn he was in the midst of some suffering himself—an older cousin of his had recently succumbed to an undisclosed illness. Of course, pleased was not the word she spoke aloud, but the honesty in his compassion was sincere, and so was the fragility in his lovemaking.

Perhaps then, coworkers with sensitivities was the better descriptor. For one another, after ten hours a day of being desensitized, they provided the proper outlet to feel again; to touch; to be touched; to for once dizzy the heart's metronome after spending so many hours keeping pace with the quartz clock that hung above their desks.

LUCKY

So one of the reasons I was a bit late tonight was, and keep this to yourself, was that Victor—you know Victor, you met him out at the dinner in February, the real tall guy, I think he was asking you about publishing?—he asked me to grab a drink after work and sort of out of nowhere he told me he was having trouble at home. It wasn't totally out of the blue, he'd hinted at it before, but it was tough, you know? Here's a guy, he never had any kids, it's been just him and his wife, and they'd made a nice life for themselves, built something up over sixteen years, and all of a sudden it's gone. And I think he's looking forward, after all those years of sort of depending on her—he never really made many friends outside of work—and what is he left with after it falls apart? I mean what do you say then, right? He's still young, he should be able to rebound, but the next year, it's going to be just incredibly hard for him. And so anyways, in between listening to him and thinking about what I could possibly say to cheer him up, I couldn't help but think of you. Think of how well we've worked it out. How fortunate I am not just to have you, but to be able to say that I'm coming home every day to the woman I love, the family I love, and it really hit home today, when Chelsea squeezed my leg when I opened the door, then I saw you, and you had those mitts on when I came to kiss you, and it's, it's everything, you know? We've done so well and yet, we're still both pretty young, and we've just got so much to look forward to. I just wanted to tell you that. That I'm lucky. Lucky to have you all. Lucky to be able to look forward to you.

UMBRELLAS

The bus was late when it started to rain. The first drops dropped not like droplets at all, but like the innards of water balloons bursting one by one upon the pavement. A minute later, the dark cloud above released its trap door and the flash flood had begun.

She had been waiting beside him, wearing a pearl-colored blouse which appeared so delicate that he doubted it could withstand the kiss of the summer sun let alone the ravaging of a spring rain. He made no hesitation, stretching his umbrella over her body before the storm could impact its worst.

"Thank you," she said. "I forgot mine at home."

The rain fell harder and before long it seemed as if the two of them stood alone within a tube of glass while the city filled around them like an aquarium. For seven minutes in all, they shared the same red canopy, blushed within the same breathless humidity, and excused themselves with each accidental glance of their shoulders.

When the bus arrived, he allowed her to board first before popping his umbrella once to dry. She chose her usual place on the bench up front and he casually found an available seat three rows back.

He could not help but to think how fortunate it had been that she, of all riders, she, the brunette with sea green eyes and perfect posture, who carried paperbacks while the world moved on to tablets, should be standing next to him without an umbrella on the morning in which it had begun to pour like no other. He allowed himself to hope that his dream of seeing her and her perfect posture in a setting other than on the bus was now a day closer to coming true.

As the bus stopped at Eighth Street, and she rose to exit, he learned the valuable lesson that the best fortunes are rarely won accidentally. For through his rain-spotted window, he saw her slender arm pull from a tote bag the brightest yellow umbrella he had ever seen.

CUE THE VIOLINS

"Cue the violins…" She said.

"What?"

"It's an expression. My Dad, whenever something really sad or sappy happened, he used to say, 'Cue the violins.' So when I was nine or ten, I randomly called him out on it. I said violins can be happy, too. And ever since, we've had this thing: 'Whenever you want to celebrate life, cue the violins.' You just kissed me. At last. Cue the violins."

THE TIME TRAVELER

And in my younger eyes, I saw the futility of time travel. In the end, it was not the science of it, nor the morality of it. No, what undermined time travel was much simpler: Love. It exists in an exact time and place. It is a single string stretched endlessly until cut or broken.

I made every effort of convincing my younger self not to walk away. With all my heart I persuaded him to remain true, but his eyes explained everything his stumbling words could not: his decision had been made and no apparition from the future would change that. A vital line had permanently been severed.

Perhaps such is the arrogance of young men, but take from it instead the nature of love: that once cut, love cannot be refashioned, not in the way it once was. Great love endures. Great love is continuous. In the end, I traveled forty-five years to push upon that delicate string. How much easier it could have been to pull from the present.

A VALID EXCUSE

"Professor Samuelsson, I don't have my assignment ready yet, but I think I have a valid excuse."

"And what is that, Charles?"

"I fell in love this weekend."

Professor Samuelsson nearly fell out of his chair. He had heard many excuses before, but none so brazen as this.

"You fell in love?"

"Yes, sir."

"And because you fell in love this weekend, you would like an extension?"

"That's correct, sir."

Professor Samuelsson burst out laughing. He couldn't help himself. "I'm sorry," he said to Charles once he regained his composure. "But if I may ask you one question: What was her name?"

"Lia," answered Charles directly, as directly as any student had ever answered him before. It was the voice of truth, Professor Samuelsson thought. Steady atop the monument of love and delivered without fear. There was no question, his student had spoken truth.

"You are excused from this assignment, Charles. In its entirety. Congratulations on your weekend."

BROS

"Dude, we got a problem."

"What's up?"

"I met her last night."

"Met who?"

"*Her*."

"Oh, no."

"Exactly."

LOVE THIS LIFE

"Love this life," he said. "That comes first. You start loving this life, and you'll have no trouble loving her. Better yet, she'll begin to notice, and when she sees how much fun you're having, it'll be contagious. Your happiness will spread from the absolute center of her heart to the very end of her fingertips. And only then, once you've begun to truly love this life, and shared it with her, will you find out what it's like to be left awestruck by how much love she was capable of in return."

GRAND CENTRAL

We fell in love that winter, alternating weekend visits between New York and Providence. It was largely for her sake that I preferred the Friday evenings which found me travelling north, but I did discover a certain therapy in those biweekly excursions. A sort of metamorphosis, the process of shedding the city and the week-that-was as I blurred past Harlem on until the fishing villages of eastern Connecticut would appear and by then the week would seem as tangible as a nearly forgotten dream. And, of course, she was there, always at the end. When life too often fails to maintain a desired direction, the feeling of hurtling towards the woman you love can never be underestimated.

It is the reverse image, however, that holds truest for me: the second and fourth Friday of each month, standing atop the north stairwell of that magnificent station. Just below, witnessing the Main Terminal at its busiest, a tide pool of marble and stone splashed again and again by endless waves of passengers. Eddies forming as suits swirled, charcoal, blue, and black, occasionally streaked by women in their ruby red dresses or floral white blouses. And yet, from the top of that stairwell, she was so easy to place. Amidst the changing currents, her beauty held still.

PAST IS PAST

He was boyfriend number fourteen, she was girlfriend number two. What to make of that number? In total years spent dating, their experience was nearly equal. But what of her history, would she quickly replace him like she had all the others? Or of his, could she at least match, speaking nothing of hopefully one day surpassing the emotional weight of his nine year relationship?

These questions had lingered over her, biting at her conscious from the moment she first compared their histories. When it became too much, she blurted them all out at once in a five-minute-long barrage, damning the consequences of maybe even being called insane.

"Well, it's probably true," he said, an answer which sent a shiver through her body. "But why don't we try to simplify it," he continued. "Do you love me?"

"Yes."

"And do you believe me when I say that I love you?"

"Yes."

"There we go, then. Glad we settled that."

DAYLIGHT

They woke by the daylight. The warmth entered the curtains and she shed the blanket from where it had been hot on her skin. He pulled his portion high onto his neck. All winter he had been cold. Too warm did not exist. What did exist was the thought that if only all mornings could begin like this: in place of the screaming dark, the gathering and gentle glow of her backside reflecting the dawn. There in the milky haze he charted a diamond, then a kite, the brown-freckled stars forming a constellation in reverse. Her perfume traced on his pillow and he remembered what it was like to chase that scent into the night and how even the darkness had a way of revealing things which light could not. Until she rolled her shoulders squarely to the mattress and he saw a beauty which he had only previously drawn with his touch. Her lips drew a blissful smile, the daylight brightened, and he was warm again.

THE CUBES

This had happened before, he thinks. A lot of girls have said they like The Cubes, but that does not mean they like *all* of their music. Mostly it's 'Harvest,' or 'Fast Food Ecstasy,' which everyone loves, but it's doubtful she's even heard of 'Thread Count,' or 'Soap Dish Blues.'

"You know what my favorite song is?" She continues. "'Thread Count.'"

Oh God, he thinks. This has happened only once before. August 2nd, 2009. Gertrude's Hall. Nell Ryland. He unsuccessfully proposed to Nell that same night.

"It's weird. It's like when I hear 'Thread Count,' no matter where I am, I am just instantly happy."

It's not weird. It's not weird at all. In fact, he knows this feeling quite well. It's like a canister of nitrous being released beside him and his heart lifts, feeling lighter with every note until the song ends and he feels like he could sometimes float away.

Yes, he knows the feeling, and yes, this has happened before. Do not propose, he reminds himself. No matter what, even if this seems like love, even if it *is* love, do not propose to her tonight. Remember what The Cubes say in 'Soap Dish Blues,'

"*You can't always wash away the dirt in the morning.*"

KEEP ME GUESSING

"I want to ask you an unfair question," she said.
"Okay."
"Can you make me fall in love with you in one night?"
"Yes," he responded. "But only on one condition."
"What's that?"
"That if I succeed, you keep me guessing. Because I don't ever want to stop working for your love."

SACRÉ-COEUR

This is their last night in Paris. Soon she will return to Los Angeles and he to New York. It seems unfair, she thinks, that they should be given only three short days after such an improbable reunion. Measured differently, though, and she would admit that there had been blocks of years which added to less. Still, it is a shame their time should end so much like a dream—with a kiss and then she wakes.

"Do you think we get third chances of love?" She asks from atop the steps of Sacré-Cœur.

"No, I think once it happens, love always exists. The question is, will we be fortunate to meet again?"

"Will we?"

"Yes, I think so. We are living proof that fortune favors those in love."

THE LOTTERY

What's that? You haven't won the lottery yet? Oh, I beg to differ. Start with being alive, being here right now, where do you place those odds? Or how about the fact that you woke up to a beautiful day, in a beautiful home, in a beautiful neighborhood. Have the odds gotten better? And let's not forget how you woke up next to a beautiful woman whom you call your wife. There are 6.9 billion people on this Earth, and you found the one who happens to find you the most handsome of all. How's that for winning a lottery? So let me ask you this—if you now agree you've won the lottery, are you smart enough to hold on to your winnings?

PORCH

"Tell me," he asks, "what is it like tonight?"

"A bit chilly," she begins, "but beautiful. The sun is starting to set to the left of the house. A minute ago a family of cardinals flew by, the crickets are making their evening conversation, and the sky, above the trees it's gold, but to the east, it's the most perfect blend of blue, like a never ending pond you wouldn't mind wading in to."

"It sounds beautiful."

"It is. I wish you could see it."

"Me, too," he replies. "But I think I would be easily distracted."

"By what?"

"By the hauntingly beautiful woman sitting on a rickety white porch swing, in sweatpants and her husband's blue windbreaker, her hair done up in a wickedly sexy new do…

"And I think, if I were there, reaching the top of those steps, and I saw the look of complete surprise on her face, I would probably miss out on the family of cardinals, the pond-like sky, or the chill in the air, because I'd see her and I'd want to tell her that I love her and that I missed her so ever, ever dearly."

THE MOST IMPORTANT THING

"Daddy, what's the most important thing you should do when you love someone?"

"Tell them," he responded. "You should always tell someone that you love them."

"More important than that!" She replied.

"Well, I guess there's lots of other things. You should try to be there for the people you love. Care for them, help them, support them…"

"Even more important!"

"I don't know then. What is the most important thing?"

"The most important thing you should do when you love someone is, you shouldn't ever get mad if they do something bad."

ST. MARKS

"Do you believe in love?" She asks. "Or do you think it's just something that we do?"

"I think it exists."

"Hmm," she responds. Her room is windowless but I can imagine her reading the ceiling in the perfect dark. Through the wall behind us, the night's circus howls on.

"Can you make me believe?" She continues a moment later. "I think I'd like to believe again."

PAYBACK

You know he burnt off my eyebrows, right? The night we met. He was trying to act all cool, going on and on about what a big stud he was on the grill, so he says, "Hey, watch this!," ignites half a gallon of lighter fluid which explodes into this massive ball of fire and singes both my eyebrows off.

Yea, I know. Lucky he didn't kill me, right?

So, understandably, I spent the next month wanting to kill him. Literally, wishing I could tie him to a propane tank and fire a shotgun at it like they do in *Jaws* or something. I even told him that the first few times he visited. I opened the door and said, "If I see you again, I'm going to kill you." But he felt so guilty about it he kept showing up, every day. And that was the thing—he showed up every morning for the next four weeks with a new wool cap or large pair of sunglasses for me to wear.

After all that, I couldn't stay mad at him. But you know me, I'm not going to forget about it, either. I always get even. Well, it took me five years, but I definitely got even…

Did you know you can get branding irons personalized?

So for his thirty-fourth birthday I get him this whole new set of bar-b-que equipment, including as a joke, or at least he thought, a branding iron with my initials.

Ha, I think I said something stupid like, "So you can think about me whenever you grill."

To finish the story, a week after his birthday, once we got our first chance to use all this stuff, I waited until he's turned around with just a pair of basketball shorts on, and I took that beautiful iron, and I branded him straight on the ass.

I'm probably lucky he didn't file domestic abuse charges, but I swear, there was nothing in my life funnier than seeing my initials branded on that big soft right cheek of his. I nearly died.

PINS AND STRINGS

Their courtship seemed to have been a perpetual crisscross from the moment they first met as members of a wedding party. They reunited a year later in the food court at JFK, spending an hour together before boarding separate flights to Brussels and London. It had been such a disappointment, they thought, considering how far they were each travelling, and how relatively close they would be in Europe. Knowing it wouldn't be quite close enough. Their third and fourth run-in's occurred within weeks of one another at separate restaurants within the West Village. Both times, they each dined with the company of dates, though she was careful to notice his date had changed the second time while hers had not. A two-and-a-half year interlude followed, during which they had nearly forgotten one another, until one day he found her carrying a lamp up the steps of a brownstone. He asked her if she was moving.

"Back to the city," she said.

"And where had you been?"

"I could ask you the same thing," she replied, "but that truck would still have furniture in it. Start lifting, then we'll catch up."

And so that night, dining atop a flipped cardboard box, they filled in the spaces of their lives, connecting the dots like strings pinned to a map. Soon they were struck as much by the near misses as the few connections they had made.

"I'm sorry I never reached out," he said at last, genuinely upset with himself.

"Don't be," she replied. "You had a life to lead."

"But you know what I mean."

"I do. And I also know that it led you here tonight."

FROM RIGHT FIELD

The other mothers sit on the bleachers exchanging their latest gossip and grievances. I do not blame them. Lord knows I have my own grievances to list but that is not why I am here. I stand along the fence in shallow right field.

Today Nick is in center field and I have an easy view of him as he chews the strings of his mitt tight, anxious for a ball to leave the infield. It is a sort of purgatory for him, he would much rather be at second base or short, but I will never speak up and nor will he. I tell him there is something to learn from every position, being part of a team not the least.

Soon he will be happier at bat again. He'll stroll to the plate looking relaxed as if he had simply gone for a walk and found himself standing within a batter's box. From there, Coach Murphy will berate him to get into his stance sooner and the pitcher will wind up, quicker than usual, convinced he's caught the batter asleep at the plate.

Only then, once the ball is released, does Nick transform. The bat will lift from his shoulder, his forearms will tighten with a flash of muscle that even I have trouble believing could come from my own son, and he'll slide his front foot forward effortlessly as if he and the ball were part of some cosmic certainty destined to meet.

The body belongs to his father. The gamesmanship, the competitor in him, that's me.

Sometimes the ball will crack off the bat so loudly the ladies will cease their conversation, and turn their heads in unison, just in time to see the ball soar over the chasing backside of one of their own in left field. The "ooh's" and "aah's" will follow and this I gladly accept as my socializing for the day.

Most of the mothers have other children. I am sympathetic. How they can differentiate the endless calendar of games, practices, and recitals is a wonder to me. They deserve this hour of peace. I only have Nick, though. Polite, serious Nick who never gave me half the trouble he was entitled to and who loves baseball more than I imagine cows love grass.

So it is that I love baseball, and why I stand in right field.

HELLO

"How did it happen? She said, 'Hello,' and I knew I would never wish to say, 'Goodbye,' again."

ALBUM NO. 2

"When you finished your album, when you saw your name on the record for the first time and you played it all the way through and heard your own voice coming from the speaker—what did you say when it was over?"

"Nothing. All I remember was being speechless."

"Like how could something you dreamed of for so long be real, right? How could it be so tangible, how strange was it to feel it in your hands and see it?"

"Surreal. Completely surreal."

"I've felt that twice now. Twice in my life."

"When you finished your record?"

"That's one."

"What was the other time?"

"When I finally kissed you."

ALL THAT MATTERS

"What's the matter, honey?"

"He doesn't like me!"

"It's all right."

"No, it's not all right."

"Sure it is."

"What do you mean, sure it is? How can it be all right? The only guy I've ever cared about, the only person I've ever opened myself to, the only person that really means anything to me—he doesn't care. He doesn't like me. And none of it matters."

"Well, I think it matters."

"What matters?"

"I think it matters that you care, because not enough people do. I think it matters that you were willing to open your heart to someone, because that's also hard to do. And I think it matters that you're learning how to value others in your life."

"Well, how does that help me?"

"It helps you because, one day, a pretty great guy is going to come calling, and he's going to care about you, he's going to open himself to you, and you're going to mean more than the entire world to him—and, can I tell you something, if you thought what you felt for this one boy was pretty special, I can tell you it's even more special when the both of you feel the same way."

COULD NOT LOVE BACK

I once loved a woman who could not love back. She could only love front. At first, I found it to be an amusing, whimsical, way to love—always facing forward, always gazing into each other's eyes, communicating our deepest affections with words rarely spoken. But soon I realized the limits of a backless love. At night, when I so often sleep on my side, I could not roll away as she would wake in tears. Or a proper goodbye, kissing her on the cheek and turning, savoring the parting as an introduction of the desire to meet again. Instead I would bumble away, stepping backwards, facing her until I could safely round a corner or duck behind a sizeable post box. In no time at all I was exhausted by the effort. More than any desire I had ever felt, I wanted to turn my back to love! Let her see me disappear with the truest faith that I would return. No doubt, I would race to her with a ready embrace and a passionate kiss. I wanted it so badly—until the day, recognizing my angst, she walked away from me forever, her backside a delicate glide over the pavement, and I realized that I, myself, would never love back again.

ANGELS

She called me an angel once. We were parked in her parents' driveway, it must have been one in the morning, and before she stepped out she told me she believed in angels and she thought I was one.

I was twenty then. I didn't believe in angels. I barely believed in what was right in front of me. To hear her call

me one, though, before she ever let slip that she loved me...
it was...

There are moments when you feel yourself elevate somewhat in experience, when you sense a sort of heightened level of understanding of this life. Here was one for me. It made no difference if I believed in angels myself. What mattered was that she did, and I would live up to it. No matter how high that standard might be, I would be her angel.

It's what I've tried to be ever since.

I think she was right, though. In angels. I still don't know how it works, if there's only some angels, or if maybe it's all of us. Maybe we're all here trying to earn our own wings. But I believe her now.

I believe they're among us. I believe there are people on this Earth who can perform miracles for others. And whether they're aware of it or not, I think there are people who help guide us along the highest paths we set for ourselves.

I believe because this is what happened to me. One night in a driveway an angel spoke to me, and ever since my path has been higher.

PEN PAL

Dear Brian,

I hope you are having fun in Buffalo. School is not as much fun without you. I have Mr. Willis. He is mean. Do you like your teacher? Everybody misses you. Kyle is really sad. He said you were his best friend. Do you have a lot of friends yet? I bet you have a lot of friends. You are really funny. Do you remember Alex B? He asked me to be his girlfriend. I told him you were my boyfriend. Will you be my boyfriend?

<3<3<3 Mary <3<3<3

(P.S. I still have the goodbye card you made me.)
(P.P.S. Write Back!!!!!!!!)

THE HIGH LINE

It had been two years since they had last seen one another. That was the night she walked out of their apartment never to return, leaving her belongings behind for a set of movers to collect. Neither could remember their parting words, but they had been filled with hate and regret—the sort of things you could never imagine saying before and would horrify the very core of you to realize you just did.

They crossed paths on the High Line ("I hadn't heard you moved down here…"). She looked stunning, wearing a new green sundress that hugged the body he knew so well. She thought him handsome, too, in a suit that suggested he had progressed exactly as she expected he would. Even when he didn't believe, she thought, she knew a good horse when she saw one.

They spoke for an hour and half, watching the sun slip between the brick warehouses on 22nd Street and down over New Jersey.

With dinner appointments waiting, they finally stood to say goodbye. He kissed her on the cheek and each took exceeding care not to miss an inch to the left—an inch that felt shockingly more recent than the two years which separated it.

As they turned away, she stopped to say, "I'm glad we have this. I missed it."

"Me too," he replied, adding, "I think we'll always have this."

RECEIPT

In his office hangs a receipt, displayed in a small oak frame:

> *Danielle's Coffee Shop*
> *05/12/03 7:32 A.M.*
> *Cashier: Heather*
> *Order #20071*
> *1 MD Coffee*
> *1 Espresso*
> *1 Pastry*
> *Total $4.79*

"What is this?" He is often asked.

"A receipt, of course."

"Why do you have it?"

"How many people have a memento from the exact moment they fell in love? Anne forgot her wallet that day. For the price of a coffee, I bought a lifetime of happiness."

ANOTHER WORD FOR ROMANCE

"Do you know what another word for romance is? Effort. A candlelit dinner is a fine setting to be sure, but what makes it romantic is the fact that you went through the effort to set the table. It's taking the extra steps to show you care. Do something for her. Take time out of your day to make her day better. That's romantic. Too many people mistake romance as needing the white horse or the shiny armor to be the knight—that was never the fairytale. The fairytale was the idea that the knight thought to save her, and did so, whether on a horse or a mule. Love, romance, relationships, they take work. Work for it a little, and you'll find your romance."

STARS

Our party ends once the fire pit reduces itself to no more than a few glowing embers. Casey opts to stay outside while I help our guests with their belongings.

Fifteen minutes later, our friends all gone home and the dishes delivered to the washer, I return to the backyard. It is much colder now, but she seems content, her neck arched to the sky.

"Are you okay?" I ask.

"Yes. But could you bring me a blanket?"

"Is that an invitation?" I ask playfully.

"You know you're always invited."

"I know," I say, and fetch her a blanket.

When I come back she has her feet pulled up on an adjacent chair. I place the blanket over her scrunched body and align two more chairs beside her.

I am a bit tipsy. Judging by her slight lisp, she is, too. But I can see the stars just fine. Here is the Big Dipper, and there the Little Dipper, together encompassing the extent of my astronomical knowledge.

"What are you thinking about?" She asks after a minute.

"Just stars," I say. "What about you?"

"Just stars," she says. "And you…"

EXERCISE #8

Stand up on a bus or other mode of public transportation and announce, "My name is (state your name) and I am in love!"

Next, look towards the passenger seated directly beside you and say, "Now it is your turn! Share with us your love!"

Continue until the entire bus has professed their love. If someone declines to participate, encourage them by saying, "Do not worry, for we love you still!"

After every passenger has had the opportunity to profess his or her love, encourage a group cheer by saying, "Together now: 'We are on a bus! And we are in love!'"

(Repeat with passengers, 'We are on a bus! And we are in love!')

Finally, say to the bus, "Thank you all for sharing your love! With thanks to YouTube, our love will now be shared with the entire world!"

THE CRAZIEST THING YOU EVER DID

"What's the craziest thing you ever did to pick up a girl?"

"Well, once I laid myself down in front of a girl's Suburban until she agreed to go to prom with me. Then in college, I got the a cappella team to sing 'Take A Look At Me Now' to this girl on her birthday. She was on a big Phil Collins kick at the time. That was pretty good. My first year out of school I started an online petition, I got twenty-thousand people to sign it, asking another girl if she would go on a date."

"Did she say yes?"

"No, that one said no. I made the mistake of putting her picture at the top of the petition. She got a lot of phone calls. But anyways, the craziest thing I've ever done. I've got it. 2008. I'm walking across 52nd street and I pass this girl, I mean just flat out gorgeous. And I see she's eyeing me, up and down, like this right, so I get a little bit of confidence, and would you believe this, I go right up to her, and I say, "I think you are the prettiest girl I have ever seen and I would marry you right here if you let me."

"And were you disappointed when I said no?"

"Not even close. I got your number didn't I?"

KEEPING SCORE

You know what I love? Life. I love it. I love waking up in the morning. I love having my cup of coffee and a couple slices of bacon. I love my wife. I love kissing my wife, telling her how beautiful she is. I love my kids. I love being surprised by what they'll do next. I love knowing that the things they'll do and see in their lifetimes will make my life look simple. I love winning. And not just by a little bit. I love running the score. Because if you honestly care about winning then you should be ashamed when you lose by double digits. And that's why I love comebacks, too. Because it means you've been beaten. You've been slapped in the face. And I'll tell you something, you show me someone that's been slapped in the face and then swings right back—that's someone who loves life. Because life'll do that to you sometimes. It'll knock you down and kick the wind out of you. But you gotta get up. I've been knocked down so many times it don't even bother me no more. Why? Because I know I'll stand right back up. You know, four years ago, I nearly died. Heart attack. Took me a minute to figure out what was going on but you know what I said? I said, "No thank you, God. Jackie's got ballet at three and the Knicks are on at seven. You can send me the invitation later." That's right. It's a crazy life, but I love it.

FAR BESIDE YOU

In the sunny summer days
When we're busy chasing rays
Sometimes I find myself
        Far from you

And I know that it's okay
Beneath the sun you're always safe
Even if I'm
        Far from you

But if the Earth starts to quake
Or the medicine won't take
I'll be there
          Right beside you

And should worst comes to worst
I won't let your bubble burst
I'll be there
          Right beside you

So take this as my promise then
No matter where our days should end
I'll always be
          Far beside you
          Far beside you
          Far beside you

NERVOUS

"It's funny, you'd think at some age you'd stop getting nervous."

"Oh my God, you really are nervous right now, aren't you?"

"Terrified."

"Ha. Can I tell you something that might help?"

"What's that?"

"I'm a little nervous, too."

A NEW MOM

I saw a picture of Sarah today, of her and her newborn. The picture is set up like one of those old Vermeer paintings: she is in a rocker, and there's a window behind her, sunlight pouring through the open curtains upon them both. I have not seen Sarah in person in many years.

When we first met, she had snuck into my dorm room claiming she was being chased by ghosts. We did not kiss, that night or any other, but she did stay with me in my bed until the sun rose. After our ghost night we became close and I learned much more about her—how her relationship with her own mother was strained, that she was deathly afraid of lightning, and that in her mind she still believed she was six. How then to cope with the world which saw her as nineteen?

Even though I have not seen her in many years, I have been kept informed through updates like these. She twice moved, settling in Denver. There she met a man by the name of David who I have not met but seems to have been the complement in this world that she needed. And now, she is a mother.

In the picture, her face is serene. There is warmth in it, a life to it that I have never witnessed in person. Afraid like the rest of us if she could ever grow up, I wonder what she would say if I were to ask her now, "Do you still feel six?" I expect she would laugh, but I know what my response would be, having seen it clearly in that picture: The six year old grew up. Maybe over several years or in one miraculous moment...

You're all grown up Sarah. And what a mother you'll be.

BACK OF THE NAPKIN

314,000,000	U.S. Population
28,908	Average Life Expectancy in Days
1	Number of Times a Person Meets the Love of Their Life
5,431	Number of Couples Who Will Meet the Loves of Their Lives Today

Is this the day for you?

STAY

This is the bay lot, where teenagers gather in the summer to sneak their thirties or disappear in back seats. Tonight the lot is empty and she sits perched on the roof of her car contemplating fate. Ahead, the bridge glistens, mirrored in the still night. That is the way out, she thinks. That is goodbye. Forever even. Behind her in the darkness is the way back in, to the island that is her life. It is as simple as that—there is a bridge out and there is an island in. He has not left the front step, she knows, where the bridge rises in full view. He'll see the taillights and imagine each set as being hers. And she hears him, like the soft spill of the bay onto the shore, she hears him say to her, "Stay."

THE LAST LOVE STORY

They say every love story has been told before. That there are no new love stories, only echoes of the past.

Let's change that. Let's make a noise so loud it drowns out the echoes. We'll make it so perfect the writers drop their pens in defeat.

The Last Love Story. Written by you and me.

SIX YEARS

Bob Rothschild   03/02/07   3:13 A.M.
Good to see you again!

Katie Mint   03/03/07   7:13 P.M.
Good to see u 2! :)

Bob Rothschild   03/03/07   9:12 P.M.
Yea, weshould all get together again soon!

Katie Mint   03/04/07   10:12 A.M.
Def!

Bob Rothschild   08/22/09   8:46 P.M.
Hey Katie — out of the blue but this reminded me of you. Hope you're well

Katie Mint 09/15/09 2:03A.M.

Hi Bob! Sorry I took so long! Don't use this much. Haha. That is funny. Do u remember that night?

Bob Rothschild 09/16/09 8:45A.M.

Ha. Yea. It was a fun night, right?

Bob Rothschild 04/10/10 9:23A.M.

Katie — I saw Beth yesterday. She said you moved to Baltimore. Hope the move is going well

Katie Mint 7/19/11 10:11P.M.

In the back!

Katie Mint 7/20/11 3:51A.M.

Yoyf aer graaty

Katie Mint 7/20/11 4:53A.M.

Sorty. Drimk.nit

Katie Mint 7/21/11 12:56P.M.

I am so sorry. I hope I didn't do anything stupid. Let's do dinner when we're sober again!

Bob Rothschild 7/21/11 4:31P.M.

Don't be sorry. I'm glad last night worked out. I'm around this weekend. My cell is 212.555.1313. Dinner would be nice

Katie Mint 8/04/11 9:12A.M.

You didn't have to do that. Thank you.

Katie Mint 11/27/11 10:19P.M.

Miss you

Bob Rothschild   2/06/12   8:45 P.M.

You're next to me right now, but for next time you see this, miss you, too.

Katie Mint   5/15/13   1:15 A.M.

Dear Bob,

I started thinking about how we first met. And then how we kept in touch on this. And I'm just so glad and thankful you kept in touch. Anyways, I know you heard me say it last night, but I wanted to write it on here, too. Yes…. yesyesyesyesyesyesyesyesyesyesyes! YES! You're the love of my life and I cannot wait to spend the rest of my life with you.

Love always,
Katie

FALLING UP

Here, I want you to try something. Lay all the way down on the grass with me, and stare up into the sky. Now look past the trees and up towards the clouds, feeling just how much space there is between you and the sky. Then look up further, beyond the clouds, and up and up as far as you can see…

Now, all of a sudden, can you start to feel that? Like you're about to fall? Like maybe you're upside down, at the very bottom of the world, and there's just barely enough gravity holding you back to stay attached to the ground, and if it were to let you go, you would fall right off this Earth?

And at the same time it's sort of great because it's not like falling to the ground where you might get hurt. You aren't scared, because maybe it wouldn't be so bad to fall into the sky, to be able to tumble through all those clouds and down towards where everything is blue.

Feels kind of funny, kind of neat, right?

Well, that's kind of how it felt like when I fell for you.

FLIGHT PLANS

"So let me get this straight," she said. "If I tell you to, you would switch your flight right this second and fly to where I live instead."

"Yes."

"And what if I left you behind when we got there?"

"I trust you."

"What about Boston? Don't you need to be home for anything?"

"Not until Monday."

"You know you're crazy, right?"

"Crazy good, or just crazy?"

"Right now, just crazy."

"Then what do I have to do to get you to say yes?"

"Okay, fine. Let's try this," she said, reaching for two napkins. "On one of these I'm going to write my flight number and on the other I'm going to write my phone number. As soon as I leave, I want you to choose just one napkin and throw the other away without looking. If you pick the flight number, I'll see you at the gate. If you get the phone number, I want you to call me at eight P.M., exactly two weeks from now, and not a moment sooner. Sound fair?"

"Very," he agreed, and turned his back so she could fill out each napkin.

When she finished, she tapped him on the shoulder and said, "It was nice meeting you. I hope we meet again soon," before turning away from the bar and potentially leaving him forever.

As soon as she was out of sight, he swung his arm towards the first napkin. In neat, bubbly print she'd written her phone number. He lunged for the second napkin, begging to learn which city was blessed enough to call her its own. There was no flight number. She'd written the same phone number twice.

And so, feeling both heartbroken and cheated, he boarded his plane to Boston alone.

Over the next two weeks he thought of her off and on, debating whether or not he should bother calling at her predetermined time. She'd already duped him once, he wasn't sure if he wanted to give her the satisfaction of doing it again.

Finally, at eight P.M. that Friday, with the benefit of a coin flip, he settled on dialing. At least it would be better to know.

"Hello?" She answered.

"Hi. It's me. From Cleveland."

"Ah, yes. So you didn't win the grand prize, did you?"

"You tricked me."

"Did I?"

"Yes, as a matter of fact."

"Well, if I recall, you weren't supposed to look at both napkins, either. But I'll play along. I'm staying at the Four Seasons this weekend. Say you pick me up about nine?"

SCAR TISSUE

"Have you ever been in love before?"

"Yes."

"Is that mean to say? The fact I like you more because you've felt it?"

"Because you have, too."

"Yes, because I have, too."

"No, that's not mean. I like comparing scars as much as anyone. You just have to be sure you can start your heart back up when you're done."

CAUGHT

Certain things get caught. I was lost when we got caught. It was cold in the parking lot.

Certain things will get caught. Well I am lost and I am waiting to be caught. Is that your car in the parking lot?

Certain things try to get caught. I finally found what I had lost, but I turned my hand and my watch got caught. A word of caution in the parking lot.

Certain things are caught before they're caught. What's lost when I was bound to be found, you turned around and I was caught. It's warm again in the parking lot.

WILLIAMSBURG

"You know what I like about it here?" She said.

"What's that?" He asked.

"I always liked feeling like I was on the cusp. Not trapped in the thing itself, but able to look out and see Manhattan and feel like I was almost there. Like I still have something to prove."

"What do you have left to prove? You're everything."

"Just the feeling, you know? I don't think I'd ever want it all."

"And what if you got it all anyways?"

"That's why I've got you. You let me know what that feels like."

INFLECTION POINT

This is not where the story starts. The story started long ago, in 1989, when a handsome Lucas and a beautiful Marie met as assistant copy editors in Chicago. It continued through the years as their friendship blossomed, and even as they blessed one another's marriages in the late nineties. Sadly, it also continues on through the next decade when each of their marriages dissolved independently—which is nearer to where we are now, except for Lucas's brief detour to London and Marie's sojourn in San Francisco. It is here that we will pick up the story, as they each return to Chicago after years apart, alone, but not lonely, and each eager to revive a thing that is not quite past in a place that unmistakably feels present. No, the story does not start here. It is merely the inflection point. For at long last, handsome Lucas and beautiful Marie are about to fall in love.

SUMMER BEGINS

She holds his ice cream cone, black cherry, as he locks the shop behind him.

"Was it this busy last year?" She asks.

"Busier this year, I think," he replies, turning to accept his cone back.

They cross the street to the boardwalk and continue north of town where the lamps turn off each night after ten P.M.

"How are your arms? Tired?" He asks once they stop along the rail at a point that seems sufficiently private.

"No, not bad. I'll be okay."

It is dark here—there is no moon and the clouds cover the stars—still, the vanilla streak on her cheek glistens. He offers her a napkin which she accepts. Ahead, invisible waves crash on the invisibly black beach.

"A buck-thirty each," he says to her proudly. "We'll be rich by the end of the summer."

In response, she grabs what she can see of him towards her and finds him well enough to kiss him. There are different types of riches, she thinks. This outweighs them all.

And so the summer begins in earnest: with the boardwalk closed and the beachgoers gone to bed, the two purveyors of sweets locked in a sweet dish of their own. Rich as can be, in love and invisible beside the black tumbling sea.

AMO ABUNDANS

Name: Elizabeth Wendy Piper
Born: July 10, 1985
Condition: Missing love valve, *amo abundans*

Case:
Well known within the heart region is the chemical-reaction center where love is created, a process which shares similarities (in processes and energy creation) to a burning star as studied astronomically. Lesser known, the love valve is a small membrane within this center which allows the body to control its output of love (~98.7% efficiency) in reaction to circumstances that include fear, shyness, a desire to conform, or, in some instances, as a matter of prudence. Ms. Piper's condition, affecting an estimated 0.10% of the population, is a lack of a love valve.

Symptoms:
Symptoms of *amo abundans* include continually radiating happiness, social magnetism, and an uncommonly high degree of empathy.

Discussion:
There is growing support within the medical community that the love valve is heading towards evolutionary obsolescence (*See*: pinky toe). Currently, abundansectomy is not an approved procedure, and as a result, to date, no known procedures have been performed. However, with continued research, this seems possible, if not likely, by the end of the decade. Arguments against approval focus mostly on social aspects as there are no known negative physical consequences from the condition. Socially, concern exists as to

whether, in fact, there is such a thing as emitting *too* much love.

Conclusion:
Physically, Ms. Piper is by all measures healthy. Socially, she is extraordinarily well regarded. In interviews, relationships with Ms. Piper are described as, "Treasured," "The best," and in one touching reference, "My living miracle." Further study is recommend, however, Ms. Piper's case seems to promote the suggested theory that the full release of love provides extraordinary health benefits while downside risks remain minor if not equally speculative. To give Ms. Piper the final word: "Love works. Let it out."

THIS NIGHT FOREVER

"What did you think? What were you hoping for?"

"This night forever. If I could take this night, and find a way to repeat it, not exactly, maybe, but continue it—the feeling of it—I would. That's what I think."

THE WOODCHIPPER

"Let me tell you something about love. It comes when we least expect it. When I met Bernadette here, she was working for Goodwin Tackle, just up there on Route 9. I'd ordered a big box of night crawlers, and they'd sent her to deliver them fresh for me.

"Now the night before we'd had this nasty old storm that took out about half the trees over here and nearly all the ones over there. That's why there ain't nothing over there. Storm knocked them down. Course I had to clean them up, so before she got here, I was over there, on the side of the house, with the woodchipper, when my hand got caught. Sucked it right in. And, as you can tell, I lost my hand.

"So, I'm sitting there, and things aren't looking too good. I'm bleeding profusely, trying to make a tourniquet with my belt, and that's when Bernadette here shows up in her van. She tied me up good, got me to the hospital, and saved my life.

"But that's why I'm always saying: You don't know when love's gonna come. That day, I lost a hand, but I gained a wife."

SHE COOKS

"So how is it?" She asked.

Brian glanced up at his lovely girlfriend who had gotten off her seat to stand literally next to him. This was her anniversary gift: a home cooked meal. Her first. She'd called it a soufflé, but that seemed like an indignity to the French. Perhaps the French also had a translation for a pooled turd—not crap, not poop, but exactly like a turd floating in a tiny tub of green liquid and surrounded by suspended onions. He looked towards her carefully—this was the woman he would one day marry. Of this he had no doubt, which meant he could expect many more turd-soufflés ahead. He swallowed quickly and washed the remaining bile down with the closest expression to pure joy he could manage.

Could this change his mind? No, not a chance. He had a reservation for life with the most beautiful woman he knew. Yes, the reservation would include far more take-out than he'd ever anticipated, but in her company even a turd-soufflé felt worthy of a Michelin star.

"Delicious," he replied. "I love it."

MIRROR

She stares at herself in the mirror that hangs from the front door as she waits. Why is it that dresses only fit perfectly in dressing rooms? At Lord & Taylor it had hugged her torso perfectly, the only part she likes about herself. Now it wants to drift wide like one of her Grannie's mumus. At least it's short, she thinks, but of course now everyone will see her He-Man soccer legs. She slides her hands into her cups, trying to lift what isn't there, and then analyzes her face. Hopefully he won't notice the red marks where she plucked. And her mascara is uneven. Her Mom hates it when she wears too much make-up, so she waited until the last minute and rushed it. Come to think of it, now *she* looks uneven, like all over her body, like her right leg might be longer and her left shoulder hunched. She hates the fact that her Dad called her beautiful before, almost like it was something Dad's are supposed to say. There is nothing beautiful in the mirror. If she could, she would rush upstairs and start all over. But it's pointless. It's too late. He will be here soon.

On the other side of the door, he stands frozen. It has been four-and-a-half minutes already, but he is too afraid to press the glowing doorbell. The most perfect girl he has ever known will answer it. What should he say?

YOU DON'T MEET
GIRLS ON THE SUBWAY

I first saw her ride the E Train in September. She looked like she'd stepped out of a magazine. I nearly asked her if she had, except

You don't meet girls on the subway.

At first, our schedules fluctuated. Within weeks, though, we synched ourselves—arriving on the same platform, at the same time, every day, even though we never spoke a word because

You don't meet girls on the subway.

There is a third woman who rides our train. Whenever I see her, we exchange pleasantries. She asked me once why I never spoke to the girl. The reason, I shared with her, was that

You don't meet girls on the subway.

"That's the dumbest thing I ever heard," she said. "Go on. Go and talk to her." And so I did.

That's how I met my girl on the subway.

DEPENDABLE

"I tested you once. Did you know that?"

"How?"

"About three months into our dating. I noticed something different—a good thing—but definitely strange, at least to me: I could depend on you. Whenever I needed you, if I asked, you showed up exactly like you said you would."

"It's just the right thing to do."

"I know you know that. But not everyone does. So anyways, I tested you on it. I wanted to see how long you could do it for, if it was real or if I'd just imagined it. What do you think the number was?"

"I don't know, ten?"

"Thirty-three. It was the night your Mom got redirected to LaGuardia."

"Well, I mean, I had to for that…"

"I wasn't mad at all! I started crying, I was so impressed. And maybe it's better that you don't know how rare that is, maybe you've never had to know the opposite, but I want you to know I love you for it. And I hope you know you can always count on me, too."

WATER TOWER

Their legs dangle from one-hundred-fifty feet in the air. Seven miles east, the three cell towers pulse red. Occasionally Greg wishes they could climb those instead, but he knows better than to ignore the churns of his stomach which keep him safe.

Maybe it's good to know when you're high enough, he thinks.

Erin leans her back against the cool tank, resting her head beneath the legs of the giant H. She scratches Greg's new haircut and begins to work on his neck. As breathtaking as the view can be, it is never the reason she comes.

Maybe it's better to keep your dreams in full reach, she thinks.

On some nights they talk never ending. Other nights scarcely at word. On this night, an amount in between—words and hands and kisses in common, aided by the occasional breeze. And no one will bother them. Not while up here.

SAFE TRAVELS

Madeleine,

I raised you to be smart; I raised you to be well-rounded, to have the endurance to succeed, and the capacity for empathy. I have no expectations for you, that was not my role. My role was to give you the kind of foundation which would allow you to set expectations for yourself. So far, you have risen to and met every challenge you have faced. Going forward, there will be many more challenges, but you are prepared for them. Learn to define for yourself what success is. Learn to define for yourself what happiness is. In the end, only you will be grading. You are capable of anything you want to achieve in this life. And finally, when it comes to love, your mother was always wiser in that department than I. She says she chose me because she found someone to believe in. That's as good as any advice I have, only, I would add, when you find that person, allow him to believe in you as much as you will believe in him. Love exists because our partners elevate us. It goes without saying, for twenty-two years, you have brought out the absolute best in me.

Safe travels,

Dad

ON A PARK BENCH

She sat beside him on a park bench. He spent the next nine minutes questioning whether this had been an invitation to speak, or simply, a girl sitting on a bench.

"You realize," she said at last, "if I were to stand up now, and walk away, you would never know, right?"

"So what do you think I should say?"

"Start with, 'Hello.' I think we'll manage from there."

A BLANK PAGE

A blank page. A million thoughts and none at the same time. How to explain the tingling feeling he still gets when he nears her after being away, or the gratitude for the mother she's been. How to remind her of the brilliance she plays down, or the dedication she offers to her any cause. Or how do you write what it's like to kiss her, even in the morning when her breath is raw and her lips stick together; that's waking, that's the sun coming up inside. Then again at night, it's the sun setting peacefully over his kingdom, except, of course, when the moon comes out to play. How do you say these things? How do you fill that great blank page with your heart?

(Just like that, just like that.)

BLUE MORPHO

Fred likes entomology. Unfortunately, girls do not always like entomology. "So, like what," they may say, "you pin dead bugs to boards and hang them on your wall?" To which he replies, "Yes," and they scrunch their noses and step six inches back with each description of how entrancingly beautiful the wings of a Menelaus Blue Morpho can be.

That is, until the day he meets Libby who happens to maintain her own excellent collection of Blue Morpho's (Both Morpho menelaus and Morpho peleides, in fact). Upon discovering Fred's hobby, she does not scrunch her nose. Rather, she steps an inch or two closer as she peppers him with questions about specimens she has yet to see.

And so this: that we are all not alike is of no cause for concern. One man's passion is another girl's plight. But it may be helpful to know that sometimes, like the mating habits of the Menelaus Blue Morpho, when we flash our own unique wings, love has a way of flying in.

NO CHARGES

"We need to know if you want to press charges."
"I do not."
"But she shot you."
"Yes."
"Twice."
"That's correct."
"In your sleep."

"Would it have changed anything had I been awake?"

"So you agree it was premeditated."

"I don't see how it would not be."

"But still, you wish to let her go?"

"Yes, sir."

"Why?"

"Because she is my wife. Because I love her, and if she felt it necessary to shoot me, I trust her."

"She said she was upset you lived."

"Officer, if not for her, I might never have lived at all."

BAG OF BONES

Son, I've broken near every bone in my body. Look at these fingers, they ain't straight. Never will be. But they work just fine. Not perfect, maybe, but they work. The body's a miraculous thing. It's made for the long run. It heals itself so we can take chances. Of course it don't feel good to bust a fibula in half, but you go and trust your body. It will heal.

Love's the same way. Hurts like hell when we break our hearts. Worse than any muscle I've ever torn. But the body heals. Yes it does. And your heart will heal, too. It's made to heal. I'd be more worried about the poor man who never broke it once. Means he never tested it. Never saw how far this bag of bones can go.

SUMMER

THE TALLEST SWING IN THE WORLD

We rode the tallest swing in the world
Ten miles high the ropes did go
And on that board we sat so close
Me the boy, and you my girl

"Count to three and then let go"
Straight on down the mountain slope
Faster than we'd ever known
As fast, we learned, as love could grow

Ditching peaks of summer snow
We reached a land of green and gold
Here is where we made our own
"There," you said, "there is home."

Reflections in the pond below
Beside our friends, the gliding gulls
You skimmed your feet and water curled
Splashing all the nearby boats

Until, at last, we once more rose
Back atop that mountain slope
To fly, a feeling, my soul now knows
To swing from heaven with you so close

NOT A DATE

This was not a date. They could not take any more dates. They had had enough of those.

So they set rules:

"No asking about where you're from."

"Or how many brothers or sisters you have."

"And, God, please don't ask me about work. Anything but work."

"No favorites either. No favorite bands, no favorite movies, no favorite books…"

"So, basically, if it sounds like a checklist question, don't ask it."

"Perfect."

They met at a tequila bar on the west side. Their initial reintroduction was justifiably awkward as they stumbled on their own rules. Every question seemed forbidden.

But they did find their first margarita helped a little bit. The arrival of another very obvious first date helped a lot bit.

"They're going through the questions!" She whisper-yelled in his ear.

"He's terrified right now. Check out his leg. Above the table, cool. Below the table, seismic shaking."

And so they fell into a rhythm. Finally, a conversation that was not a checklist and not a reach into the psychological files of their pasts. It was entirely present—comfortably woven within the tequila bar, its patrons and concoctions, and the two beautiful faces they each saw across an unsteady wooden table.

Nights pass like this. Not by what is said, but how it's said. With joy, with humor, and with gladness that another soul would partake in the same.

It was the sort of conversation friends might have.

Until the night ended and the parameters of the evening crashed all at once.

"I have a question," he spoke beside the A/C/E entrance. "If this was not a date, then am I not allowed to kiss you right now?"

"You're allowed," she said. "I'll just pretend to not walk away."

WHAT BECAME OF A WHIMSY

It began as a whimsy, a flyer. Long time acquaintances, he had always liked her, and unbeknownst to him, she had fancied him, as well. Out of the blue he asked if she might like to get together sometime—for a drink or maybe dinner. She accepted and soon an open Thursday evening rolled into an enjoyable Saturday night. In the weeks that followed, they began to see one another more regularly, until more or less officially, they became a couple.

It was at this point the learning process really began. How little of one another had they known, how much more was there to learn? Was she really this wonderful? Was he this miraculous? Why had they waited so long to find out?

And so, as they say, what became of a whimsy, was in fact, love.

THE GOOD STUFF

They told me to write it here. All my pain. Everything that hurts. Send it here. And then I would be free.

I don't think they understand, though. It's not pain. Not the memories, at least. It's only joy. It's him. It's our time together. It's the day we met, and even the single fighting day we had that I can remember. It's our kisses, it's our traveling; it's our being lazy on a Friday night, stretched on the sofa with the red blanket and a movie. There's no pain there. Only the good stuff. The stuff I don't want to let go of. And maybe that's a reason to write. To get all the good stuff down.

But the pain...there is no pain. Only that I wish he were here. That's not pain, though. And no one hurt, and I don't hurt. It's just wanting more of the good stuff. He didn't get enough of the good stuff.

SOLSTICE

All that's lost is darkness; I have forgotten it like a fading dream. Here, there is only light and shadows emit brightness. I do not shield my eyes, nor will I shy away from the mystic glare, for she is there. Standing still at the apex of all I believe, she is there. And blinded I may be, my days are never ending. In these memories of her standing still, I'll have only forgotten darkness. This is my love in the solstice.

HAPPY MONDAY

"...it was okay. How was your weekend?"

"Amazing, actually."

"You serious? What happened?"

"Everything. Seriously, everything. Started Friday night in Brooklyn, ate at The Fifth Story which is that new roof deck place which was phenomenal and got to see the sun set over Manhattan. Went out, hit four different bars, actually met Wes Dingle from The Cubes at the last one, and eventually made it back to Hoboken in time to see the sun rise again over Manhattan. Then on Saturday, I had lunch with a bestselling author, ate dogs at Yankee Stadium for dinner, and managed to catch The Sharkoons at Bowery where, are you ready for this, we met Wes Dingle backstage for a second time and ended up riding down to A.C. with him and The Sharkoons, catching sunrise this time outside of Revel overlooking the ocean. Sunday, I hop-skipped my way north, stopping in Manasquan, and was back in Hoboken bar-b-que'ing last night by six."

"That is a pretty good weekend."

"I know, right. And I didn't even tell you the best part."

"What else happened?"

"I think I met a girl and fell in love."

SLEEPOVER

They had their jammies, they had their flashlights (matching yellow-plastic Everlast-brand). They had *The Little Mermaid* and they had lava to avoid. Tents and castles and islands and a time out to an ordinary kitchen with ordinary juice which gave them superpowers as soon as they reached the basement—go. They had lights out and glow-in-the-dark stars, and sleeping bags within which shuffling legs ignited a static storm. And they had a bed time ignored as the sleeping bags grew hot and the flashlights made creatures with spots. A pillow fight, a scary story, and....

...at last, he grew too tired, and fell to sleep.

She flashed her light on and off to wake him. Once he gurgled, but would not wake.

So she flashed her light on and off again in his face.

Still, he did not wake.

And on. And off.

And on.

And off.

It was not like she was afraid of the dark, not like he would have been. But there was an impulse of the kind she would never have understood—

To turn the light

on

and to turn the light

off

and know he was still there...

DANCE WITH MAGGIE

"Dance with Maggie," she said. And dance we did, all through the night. Even after they unplugged the microphone and the line formed to say goodbye, we made use of that empty floor, discovering an encore of melodies no others could hear.

I wish that I could dance with her some more, but I'll have to wait. One day we will exhaust the band again and she'll fall into my arms only to twirl away, spinning and spinning.

"Dance with Maggie," she said. And I'm so glad I did. Remember that, Maggie, you have a dance here waiting.

When you're good and ready, take my hand again. Pull me inside our circle of friends, and pull me forward to dance again.

PILLOW TALK

"Wait until the press gets a hold of this."

"It's only a matter of time."

"We really should go public, don't you think?"

"I do."

"They'll eat us alive."

"Yes, they will."

"I can see the headline on Drudge, 'Leaders of the Free World in Bed.'"

"Worse, 'Pillow Talk,' our heads cartoonishly large on some adult film stars' bodies."

"You can throw re-election out the window."

"But it's not illegal."

"No, it's not illegal."

"Do you regret it sometimes? Wished we hadn't?"

"No. Do you?"

"Not at all."

"It will be for the history books, that's for sure."

"But can I say something? Am I crazy to believe this might actually work?"

"Do you think?"

"Yes, I think, if you believe in our two countries like I know you do, then yes, I think it absolutely can work. It's a love story for the twenty-first century: Two single parents finding one another. That we happen to be President and Prime Minister…it might give them something to believe in."

"And if they don't?"

"Well, there's always executive powers…"

JUST ANOTHER LOVE STORY

It was just another love story: two players, a chance encounter, and that elusive benefit known as mutual attraction.

Encouraging a first date which began typically, shy and nervous, and ended under the thrilling spell of discovery that inspires second dates.

Third date and more dates, familiarity seeping in, until before long, the two players became one—a couple. Together here, together there, and everywhere together. Happy as a pair and so it should be.

Now it was undeniable, this was no passing fling. It was made of the stuff that lasts, that little four-letter word which exists so that all good things might last, onwards past every ever after. And ever this did.

Yes, it was just another love story. The same as told over and over again.

Indeed, just another love story, the same old he met him.

CEREMONY

Anne and Bobby, before we begin, please take a moment to glance about you, acknowledge your loved ones gathered here today. That is one of the blessings of a wedding, so rarely do we have that opportunity to congregate the most important people in our lives in a single setting. Be warmed by this, remember this.

Now I want to ask you a strange question. Do you think you chose these people? In loving them, was it ever a choice?

Anne, I see your mother just behind you. Do you think it was ever a choice to love her? Or beside you, Bobby, you have chosen your very closest friend, Ted, to be your Best Man today. But loving him as your friend, was that a choice?

I ask you: Do we really choose any of these people? Do we wake up one day and say, "Yes, today I will decide to love Aunt Angelica. She has always been extraordinarily kind and extraordinarily generous with her time. Today I will love her."

And the answer is: Of course not. We love these people because it is innate. It is inside of us. We can describe this as God's will or His choice. We could even describe it as something more carnal, that need to have others in our lives, the wanting to share this life with those who give it life to us.

What would be difficult, however, is to describe love as a choice. We love, and that is unconditional, even to ourselves.

Four and a half years ago, Anne, you sat down in a crowded movie theater beside a handsome young man you had never met: Bobby. We know a spilled Coke played a part, but from that evening forward, under any definition, the decision was clear. You would love Bobby, and Bobby would love you.

So now that we stand here feeling entirely bound to this moment, even destined perhaps, what hope do we have that we can choose the correct future for ourselves?

And that is what I would like to suggest to you today. That it is not *whom* we love that is among life's great choices, but *how* we love.

Together, your love brought us safely to this church. It is the miracle which will stand as the foundation for what lies ahead, both as the fire that propels you forward through life and the map which will eternally guide you. Love is the constant.

It is *how* you love, though, which will determine whether you reach the high places you seek. If love is the constant, then the *action* of love is the variable.

And that is the question you should be asking yourselves today, and with God's grace, for all the many years to come. That you love one another is a given, that is the miracle we celebrate with you. But how will you celebrate that love with each other?

Bobby, one day, you may come home from a very difficult day at the office, and you may open the door to the sound of an infant crying, or for those parents in this church, shrilling. What choices will you make in that moment to show your love not just for your child, but for Anne, as well?

And Anne, your entrepreneurship has allowed you to build a thriving business from within your very home. A blessing, for many, but in that same moment, a curse, perhaps. Amidst that deafening shrill, when all you would like to do is finish that one last task, what choices will you make?

A marriage is filled with choices. Let each of those choices reflect the love we see here today.

It is not always enough to say, "I love you." Remember, that is the given. Show one another how well you love. Honor your love with actions. Foster your love. This is the choice being handed to you today.

And together, with every single person in this church with whom you now have absolutely no choice but to love unconditionally, we wish you both a lifetime of happiness together. Let all of our choices reflect that so we can each help Anne and Bobby to remain as happy as they are at this very moment.

Congratulations, and may God bless you both.

I LIKE YOU

"I like you," she said. I'll always remember that, the way she added it to the end of the night, like a delicate punctuation. As if to say, "Goodnight, this first chapter is over, and by the way, it ended well, and if you turn the page in the morning, you'll find another chapter waiting."

Of course there were more chapters to follow. And not too far down the road they included the words, "I love you," but it's those first words I'll never forget. Her simple gesture. A brave, first step taken.

"I like you," she said.

It was all I needed to hear.

FRONT ROW SEAT

"No one came," she said, packing her guitar into her case.

"That's not true," he responded. "There were a couple of people over there before. And that guy stayed."

"I think he's asleep."

"Well he's still here. Bartender, too. The bartender stayed."

"Stop it. No one came. Do you think I'm wasting my time?"

"No. Do you?"

"Sometimes."

"What would it take for you to change your mind then?"

"You mean how many people?"

"No, what would make you stop singing?"

"I couldn't."

"Then you're not wasting your time."

"I know, but I am wasting yours. I feel bad. We could have done this from home."

"Trust me, one day you're going to be so famous you won't have any time for me between all your screaming fans. You can feel bad for me then. Not now, though. I just got a front row seat."

WHILE THE FIRE WORKS

While the fire works
While the sky burns in peace
Take a moment
Please pause and see
An entire nation
At once caught in sync

As red, white, and blue blazes
Illuminate beautiful faces
Of fathers and mothers
Sons and daughters
Lovers, neighbors, strangers in kind
Here, for a moment, paused in time

This is the fire working
Beneath blazing symbols
Of freedom, love, and peace
This is the fire working
An entire nation able
To be free, in love, and at peace

BEGIN

This is the night: This is the night they kiss. This is the night they go even further. This is the night when the walls collapse, inhibitions disappear, and they see each other for everything they are and everything they may not be. And miraculously, considering the level of reveal, considering the nakedness, considering that nothing should be left to the imagination, tonight also happens to be the night they start from scratch. Tonight is the night their imaginations take a time out and their presumptions lay to sleep. Tonight is the night they begin, for the first time really, to meet one another, to understand one another; to learn that the ideal they each built up on that first date, and thoroughly maintained, is not at all the person beside them now, but rather someone so much better.

Tonight, they'll learn everything, only to learn they know nothing.

What a wonderful place to begin.

THE ESCAPE

"If you help me escape tonight," she said. "I'll love you forever."

So we planned her breakout. It was daring and calculated. At exactly twelve-twelve (her lucky number twice), I would arrive at the base of her bathroom window on the dark side of the house with a twenty-foot ladder. She would climb out and I would race her to safety.

The night would be hers at last. Her parents would never know.

The escape was faultless. I circled extra wide of the house to avoid detection, stumbling only once beneath the weight of the ladder I had carried nearly a mile-and-a-half. At twelve-twelve exactly, I planted the ladder beneath her perch. She opened the window, stretching out like a princess in a fairy tale.

"I made it!" I shouted in a whisper.

She shushed me from above and began her descent. I wanted to rush up to carry her down, but I knew my limitations and the noise it could make. So I waited as my fair maiden descended.

Finally we were in one another's arms, embraced the way poets dream about—of freedom, triumph, and young love. As if all the hope in the world could wrap itself within a pair of teenagers breaking free.

This was our chance, our turn to capture the night.

"Which way?" I asked, anxious to learn which direction fate would lead.

"Wait," she said. "I thought you knew where Josh lived?"

ONCE

"How many times do I have to do this? How many times do I have to fall in love?"

"That's up to you. As many as it takes, if you want to succeed."

"How many times do I have to get hurt, though? Or worse, hurt somebody else. I don't want to hurt anybody else."

"Again, as many as it takes. They will grow and so will you."

"But, see, you don't even know. You can't even guess a number."

"Sure I can. Once."

"What?"

"Once. It's the same beautiful truth behind every success: It doesn't matter how many times you fail, you only have to be right once."

THE AIRBORNE LOVE EVENT

The cloud approached the city with a calmness which defied the wrath it would soon impose. Its color was rosy pink, which, were it dusk, you would question as being no more than a pleasant sign at the end of a very pleasant day. Only, when the rosy pink cloud approached the city, the time was nearer to noon.

Its first rain drops were a refreshing welcome to those in the park. The day had been a scorcher, the air hanging thick like a wet towel which until now could not be rung. In unison it seemed, the many park goers tilted their heads to the pink sky, eager to accept whatever faint relief might fall upon them. Of course, they could hardly expect the chemistry of this pink rain to include a nearly 100% efficient aphrodisiac.

Symptoms were quick and severe—the widespread sudden removal of clothing and a banshee's cry as complete strangers raced towards one another to fornicate. Near Strawberry Fields, a horseback policeman and his female partner grappled one another. Beside them, their horses already mounting or mounted. Rollerbladers, with knee pads and wrist pads still fastened, marvelously co-existed with their natural-enemy cyclists, helmets and all. Or, as occurred in the pond, an incident too vulgar to be described, other than to say it was indeed impressive in its scale and that softball players are more proficient swimmers than might generally be understood.

Until, at last, the cloud passed and the park, left savaged as if a weeklong freedom festival had come and gone within a span of nine minutes, returned to normal, and the cyclists and the bladers, the mounted policemen and their partners, the lovers in the fields, and the co-ed softball teams all awoke from their hypnosis, bashfully buttoned themselves, and returned to their summer day.

THE WELL

"Where do you draw your inspiration from?"
"The same place as most anyone else, I guess. A girl."

BROWNSTONE

His phone buzzes. "5 more min," reads her text.

She is already an hour and a half late. The Sharkoons have to be finishing up by now. Catching The Cubes' intro is a distant wish.

So he sits again and watches the neighborhood some more. Across the street, the elderly couple who had taken their collie for a walk when he first arrived with the sun still out now returns under lamplight. A cab whizzes by, the first he's seen in twenty minutes. If only she were here, he could have stopped it.

"Hey," she says from behind him. He swivels his head and the light above her falls like a halo around her slender shoulders. She swivels her foot into a small curtsey, almost to say "What do you think?"

This is the bargain. That is what he thinks. Nearly two hours of frustration, immediately forgiven. Dates with angels will always be forgiven.

YOU

(yoo)

Pronoun

1. The subject(s) being addressed by a speaker. 2. A broad reference to one or oneself. 3. Used emotively to describe a nearly incomprehensible level of infatuation, often breathless in delivery and practically singular if compared to a list of all time great loves, were such a list to exist: *You. Just you.*

HEAT LIGHTNING

I find her on the beach. In the distance, heat lightning dances between clouds, giving form to the night's horizon.

She will not apologize, I know, but neither will I. This seems to be our method instead. Always find each other afterwards. No words necessary, just finding.

Thankfully, finding her is easy. She tends to hide where it's beautiful.

I dig my feet into the wet sand and she leans her head onto my shoulder. Ahead, in silent flashes, the storm steadily approaches. It will arrive with greater noise within the hour.

By then we'll be safely inside again, once more well forgiven.

MAINE

Mistakes have been made
But I'll keep coming the same
Like the trickling waves
At the end of the bay

Some mistakes you make
For others you wait
Spent so much time waiting
It seems such a shame

It's only long distance
When love fades away
It's such a short distance
My love, stay

Oh, my love, stay
Oh, my love, stay
Stay, my love, stay

She said, "Come to Maine,
I'll be glad you came."
But I'll gladder still

She said, "Come to Maine,
I'll be glad you came."
But I'll be gladder still

THE SUBJECTIVE DETECTIVE

In her whole, as presented to him, Audrey Sleight offered the solution to the stolen locket, the burned down Cotton Estate, and the unexplained death of Mr. Chalmers. And yet, it was her whole which Pickens could not connect—too lost was he in the depths of her arctic blue eyes, too aware was he of her palm pressed to his.

In the pieces of his infatuated mind, Audrey remained a mystery, an enigma. Audrey, whom he assumed to be named after the icon of icons, yet shared a near perfect resemblance with Ingrid Bergman. Both stunning and perplexing the same way that a girl born in November could be fittingly named April.

Had she not bewildered him so, had he treated her as objectively as his job required him to, he may have noticed the black char on the sleeve of her white coat, the golden locket that hung plainly above her breast, and pursed lips nearly eager to share that "Poor Mr. Chalmers" had been anything but to her.

HOBOKEN

"I don't go into the city anymore," she said, with both of her hands resting on the black iron rail alongside the Hudson.

She never added any more than that. Instead, there was only the soft splash of the current against the pier and the barely traceable hum of the city across the river, maybe even imagined, the way that objects so large and full of life must at least hum in our minds to exist.

Of course I wanted to ask her why, but I knew better. We all have our own ghosts chasing and we each see something different in those monumental lights.

"Kiss me," she spoke at last, pulling me towards her and answering my remaining questions. The worthwhile ones, that is—the questions which look forward. All of them, answered with a kiss.

Afterwards, as she slipped quietly from the rail, leading my hand without turning back, I saw the Empire State Building dim for the night. And though I know it seems unlikely, I could not help but think maybe this had been the single moment in Manhattan's history in which it conceded to believe that, for once, a light had burned brighter from the other side.

SMILE!

Smile! For you have found love! Now race to your love and be happy.

And if you have not yet found love, smile twice more! For someone is smiling in anticipation of loving you!

ANNIVERSARY

On the morning of their twentieth anniversary, he woke her to the surprise that they would drive to Newport and visit the same bed and breakfast as they had stayed in during their honeymoon.

The day went spectacularly. They arrived in time for a lobster roll lunch, completed the Coast Walk, and returned to town so she could shop. Afterwards, they enjoyed a sunset boat cruise before dinner in the harbor. A bottle of wine on the porch deck followed, and finally, at the end of the night, in the same room as twenty years before, they made love once more.

Now she is fast asleep and he lies awake just as he had that first night. It is as if he could blink his eyes and be there again—in this same bed beside her, twenty-six then, restless with excitement, of course, but restless with nerves, as well. In a single day his life had changed, more so than any day prior. His life was no longer his, but hers.

With health and good grace, there will be another twenty years. Will this inn still be here?

He has heard of midlife crises, the panic of a lifetime rushing by, but he wonders what term they use when instead of a crisis, there is only satisfaction, only appreciation. These have been a heavenly twenty years. It hardly seems possible that the time between two blinks could be filled with so much love or such wonderful fortune.

He kisses his wife twice: once for the first twenty years, and a second time for the twenty to come. This midlife peace, he decides. This midlife peace.

ALFRED MOST

One day Alfred Most was riding the subway when he noticed an attractive girl sitting across from him. She had a tote bag wrapped around her shoulder and a name tag pinned to her shirt that read, "Ms. Utiful." Catching Alfred's gaze, she offered an extremely pleasant smile which he returned kindly while a rabble of butterflies swarmed within his belly.

At 42nd Street station, a mother entered the car with three children. The girl, who had been seated in the center of an open bench, stood quickly and approached Alfred.

"May I?" she asked excitedly, pointing to the open seat beside him.

"Of course," answered Alfred, equally excited.

As the car accelerated again, the girl pulled a book from her tote bag and began to lean deliberately in towards Alfred so that their arms touched.

"Ah," spoke Alfred suddenly. "*All My Friends Are Going to Be Strangers*. What a good book!"

"You've read it!" The girl answered, beyond pleased.

"Yes. Larry McMurtry. One of my favorites." He could not believe the odds. Unbelievable, really. His heart raced more than ever.

"I'm Bea," she continued, wasting no time.

"Nice to meet you, Bea. I'm Alfred."

"It's very nice to meet you, as well," she answered, manufacturing the perfect glow.

A moment later, the train screeched to a halt, driving Bea's shoulder into Alfred's sturdy arm. Bea felt a thrill inside her, Alfred's nerves tangled.

"Well," he spoke nervously as the doors opened, "I hope you enjoy the book!" And he raced off the subway car without remembering to ask for Bea's phone number.

Don't be like Alfred. When life hands you love, make the most of it.

DAD'S ADVICE

"What do you think, Dad?"

"You're right, it is a good opportunity."

"It's really good."

"And you'll probably make out very well."

"I'm trying to be balanced about it, but yeah, extremely well."

"It would be the proverbial icing on your professional cake, wouldn't it?"

"Yeah."

"So then what's the alternative? You stay where you are, in a beautiful home, in a beautiful town, along with your beautiful wife. A place and situation where, correct me if I'm wrong, you're quite happy, am I right?"

"You are right."

"Well, it does sound like a difficult decision, but I'll tell you this—even after promotions, I've never had a job I missed. But I did miss a lot of days with my beautiful wife, and my beautiful family, in my beautiful home.

"You've done well, son. Everything you've needed to do to get ahead. You have to decide for yourself, but if you want my advice, that's it. Don't mess with happy."

SMALL VICTORY

This is a little before *Playground* took off. I was doing pretty well, kind of grinding along, and even, you don't want to admit this, but feeling close, like I was on the verge of something pretty big, you know? Kind of sensing it…

But it's inevitable, I think, at that point, and different points along the way, when those doubts start to creep in. When you're feeling like you've been working hard, like you've been doing all the right things, but for whatever reason you're not getting the right results or the right traction.

So I knew I was close, I just felt like I needed some kind of win at the time, just a small victory to get me over the hump.

She was my win. After we met, it was like a rocket. Straight on up.

A LITTLE WHILE LONGER

"I guess timing was never our thing, was it?"

"No, I guess not."

"It helps, though, doesn't it? Knowing we have each other to care?"

"It does."

"And you know I'll always care."

"I know."

"Even if…"

"I know."

"So what is there to say then? Not goodbye, I hope?"

"No, not goodbye."

"And not 'In another life.' I don't think I could say that and mean it."

"Ha, no. Not that either."

"Then what?"

"How about you hold my hand for a little while longer and we don't say anything at all."

BED TIME STORY

"Tell me a bed time story."

"A bed time story? Jeez, it's been a long time since…"

"Try."

"Okay. Well, how about this one:

"Once upon a time, there was a beautiful maiden who lived all the way up on the fourth floor of a great tower which sat right above a Gristedes on this magical road known as 96th Street. Amazingly, she had come to this great tower, all by herself, from an enchanted and far away land called Red Bank, because, you see, she also had a magical power. This beautiful maiden had the ability to save people, very sick people—the kind of sick that can only be cured by a miracle.

"Every day she traveled from her high tower above Gristedes to this wondrous building where miracles happen, Memorial Sloane-Kettering. There she used her special gifts to help the sick find hope. Even the hope they thought they had lost, she had the ability to bundle it up for them and hand it back to them. So it was that this beautiful maiden became the hero of her very own fairytale.

"But that's not all, of course, even heroes need a little bit of help. Now do you remember how I said 96th Street was a magical place? Well, it just so happens that miracles aren't entirely free and you have to go to special places to get them. 96th Street is one of those places. The legend says that in order to perform a single miracle, you need to be kissed ninety-six times on 96th Street.

"This is where our story finishes: with a young accountant who travelled all the way to 96th Street to find this beautiful miracle maiden, and promised her as many kisses as she would ever need. Ninety-six kisses, ninety-six times over if she asked. And thanks to those kisses, and thanks to their love, all those people—the sick and the healthy—each of them filled with hope, lived happily ever after."

LOVE TRIANGLE

Q: What did the equilateral triangle say to the isosceles triangle?
A: You're the right one for me.

THE CAMPAIGN

He began a $20 million campaign to find her because, quite frankly, when you're twenty-eight years old and worth one-point-six-billion dollars thanks to a half-assed idea that happened to take off, why wouldn't you?

TV spots, billboards, banner ads, the works. He even set up a call center in Delaware to screen the incoming calls.

She had just gotten off the Pulaski Skyway, bound for the Holland Tunnel when she saw one of the billboards.

"Karen—we met on July 11th at Wilfie & Nell. Your friend felt sick and you had to leave. I'd still like to buy you dinner. Please call 1-555-4CH-ANCE."

At first she laughed, finding it funny that someone would go through so much trouble. Then she smiled, happy to share this special girl's name. She nearly caused a pile-up at the mouth of the tunnel when she realized the sign was for her.

It is a $10.25 toll and a one hour round trip through the Holland Tunnel. Karen circled anyways, caring not one bit that she was already late for work.

Dialing the number, a pleasant woman named Pam answered.

"Do you have a possible lead for Mr. Stockton?" Asked Pam.

"It's me," Karen said. "It's definitely me."

Three minutes later, she was swept through to his cell phone.

"Did I really find you, Karen?"

"Yes, you did."

"And would you like to go to dinner?"

"I think so, but…"

"But what?"

"Why? Why all the trouble? Is it crazy, or are you crazy, or maybe I am now…"

"You're not crazy. And, yes, this is crazy."

"Then why?"

"Because I believe in trying, I believe in taking chances, and to be honest with you, for the first time since I thought to do this, now that you've called, I think this might actually be crazy enough to work."

BLANKET

My mother taught me to knit. It is a skill I do not market as my own, and perhaps in part because of it I made extra certain that I could always hit a baseball further than any of my peers—sometimes a parking lot further. But knitting she taught me, suggesting to my clueless seven year old self that a blanket was the purest symbol of love. One day, she professed, I would find love, and with receipt of a blanket I would seal it forever.

Zoe and I met in junior college. We did not date until seven years later, however. In that time, I made a half-dozen girlfriends, none of which became privy to my secret skill. If they ever saw a blanket nearby, my mother served amply as a scapegoat.

I gave Zoe her first blanket on our first anniversary of dating, an August day which, if I remember correctly, broke ninety-five degrees.

"Who made it?" She asked.

"I did," I said, physically teetering on my seat. I feared my gig was up, that I had just dismantled whatever ideal I had built up with this revelation of my all-too feminine pastime.

Zoe did not bat an eye. Instead she pulled the blanket in tight and said, "So now I can always keep you close."

Since then, I have made Zoe many more blankets. Our girls joke that they have become a wardrobe piece:

"There goes Mom, with her Kate Spade and a blanket by Dad."

And then I am reminded of Mom who saw the importance of teaching her son to knit and am forever grateful—for she knew the purest symbol of love, and it wraps my love still.

LOVE IS EASY

"What's the matter here?"

"She's having love problems. Maybe you can help by telling her how hard it can be sometimes?"

"Hard? Love's not hard. Life is hard. Love is easy. You find somebody, you love them. That's it. Don't think too much. Why do you think those arranged marriages work so well? Your grandfather: I knew him to be a nice boy, I knew he worked hard, he could take care of me. Sure we were young, but we didn't think about it, we got married. Look at us now. We did pretty good, don't you think?"

"Mom, please don't suggest to her she should get married. She's sixteen."

"I was seventeen when I got married. You bet I was thinking about it at sixteen."

"You told me to wait until I was twenty-five."

"I didn't like that boy."

"And you don't know this boy."

"No, but if she finds love she should enjoy it. Not cry over it. I cried over too many things in my life. But not love. I never cried a sad tear over love."

THE ABBREVIATED ADVENTURES
OF SIR COLIN PUCKETT

The initial account of my adventures spread nearly nine-hundred pages, a trivial figure to me yet representing something just shy of life-affirming to my editor, a tiny man with tiny glasses who seems to find the miraculous in nearly everything and, I doubt, has ever experienced something truly miraculous, at least on the scale of mountains and planets and our utter failure to truly comprehend their actual size, much less meaning.

I did not enjoy knowing my life could be condensed into something so small it could fit into a rucksack. Worse, it seemed to me that the only type of person who might gather any real worth from my memoirs—primarily, young explorers in training—would hardly wish to read them. On, one, account of its length, and, two, any explorer worth the soles of his boots seeks his own adventure, not the guideposts left by others.

And so, with a bottle of McClain '22 in hand, I toasted twice. Once to the fortunate life I have lived, and a second time to that editor, a Mr. Wilkins if you wish to send sympathies, and tossed the manuscript into a well fueled fire.

Now, with that matter attended to, I present a condensed version of my adventures. All that ought to be known and can be taught, as far as I can see it. The rest, dear explorer, is for you to discover yourself:

At five thousand meters above sea level, your life belongs to your Sherpa. At only five hundred meters below, your life belongs to your vessel. Between the two, your life belongs to the woman you love. Remember this, and any adventure can be yours.

THE GREAT DIVIDE

One-hundred-thirty feet separate their desks. The view is directly across and their middle-of-the-building offices are virtual mirror images, right down to the shelf/desk that hangs on each of their eastern facing walls. It has been fourteen months since they first made contact. Of course, she took notice on his very first day in February.

They are remarkably familiar with one another. As in, their schedule: he arrives before her and leaves earlier, too. Or their lunch habits: her salads and smoothies utilize the entire color spectrum while his wraps maintain the color of a paper bag. Other habits: she always seems to have one foot raised and only clips her nails after biting them. He compulsively can have no more than four objects on his desk at one time and, yes, occasionally picks his nose. They leave Post-It notes for one another. It worries him slightly that she can read the equivalent of a 12-pt font from this distance, not knowing of course what else her hawk eyes might catch onto, his internet habits not the least of which. If they each have a conference call, they will sometimes pretend it is the same and act out with exaggerated versions of, "Is she serious?," "Shoot me," and her favorite, the "Half-awake/Half-asleep Head Bob," where she slowly slides her head lower and lower until her nose punches the "H" key on her keyboard and she cartoonishly snaps back, waggles her face side to side in a display of absolute alertness, and then repeats the process again over an approximately two-minute long cycle. If pressed to describe it, he would suggest their relationship is like one he might have with a really close colleague out of California, only opposite. Instead of trying to put a face to a name, he knows her face so well, but has yet to hear her voice. She would compare it to standing on the opposite side of a canyon abyss. On random occasions, they wave.

It is four o'clock on a dull August afternoon when she rushes out for an early date with a girlfriend who just yesterday learned she was not only being promoted, but also was asked by her boyfriend of five years to move in with him. This is a big deal.

In her rush, she does not glance towards the window, does not lock her computer, does not even say goodbye to Mindy next door. Straight to the elevator she goes, thirty-four stories down, exiting on the 48th Street side heading south where the light is green for cross town traffic and she stops.

He is there, across the street, less than one-hundred-thirty feet away. There is not a window between them.

The light turns to red, the pedestrian figure flashes green.

He starts directly towards her. She stands frozen. This is the bottom of the canyon abyss.

"I'm Kevin," he says, reaching her.

"Erin," she answers, not sure if she should take his hand, embrace him, or make no contact at all. It feels like such a strange distance to cross.

"You always seemed so far away," she continues.

"Did you think we'd ever meet?" He asks.

"I did. Or, at least, I hoped so."

"I hoped so, too," he replies. "I hoped so, too."

GOODNIGHT

"Goodnight," she says from her doorstep, turning him away just as she had on the five previous occasions.

"Sleep tight," he replies with a patient smile, and begins down the stairs.

Turned around, he does not see her remain by the door.

"How come you haven't asked yet?" She says. "Most guys would have said something or given up by now."

"It's not my place," he answers from the sidewalk.

"But you've wondered."

"Yes, I've wondered. But we all have our reasons. I can't control that. All I can do is offer you the best evening possible, which I hope I have."

"You did."

"And I'd be glad to do it again. Goodnight, Heather."

MEMORIES

I took time to think about memories today. The treasures I carry with me wherever I go. The ones that remind me of who I am, where I've been, and whom I love. Said better, why I love—things I'll hardly ever forget, like how you arrived that night in Pittsburgh and it's never been a question since. Some people do things for love, hoping, and some people do things for love, determined. You needed no hope at all, I've been at your mercy ever since.

I think about what I will remember years from now, when my head will seem like a storage bin with no roof, open to the elements and stuffed full of inconsequential items, wanting only to retrieve a single priceless antique of yesterday. Predominantly, I hope as much as I fear—is my memory strong enough, can I do enough to maintain, or is it possible to solidify my mind, so that when I grow old, and everything else has been forgotten, could I be so lucky that all I remember is you?

THE RED SCARF

The Red Scarf
J. Crew brand, 2012
On loan to the Smithsonian from Gregory and Britt Esche
The Artifacts of Today Exhibition

How can a single scarf change two lives and cause a country to fall in love? When a beautiful girl departs a Greyhound bus in Baltimore without her favorite accessory, and its finder, a man she had spoken to for only five minutes in New York City's Port Authority Bus Terminal, travels nearly three thousand miles to return it. This is the red scarf that Britt Kelsey left behind and Gregory Esche journeyed cross-country with, receiving national media attention for his search as well as inspiring a best-selling memoir, *The Red Scarf*, and its 2014 film adaptation starring Valerie Linden and Jesse Harris.

LETTERS FROM CAMP

Dear Mom and Dad,

Camp has been a lot of fun this year. I like my cabin a lot. The girls are really nice and they all think I am really pretty. Tara is my favorite. She is from Racine and she is really funny. We hang out a lot. My counsler is named Sam but she is a girl. She is ok. She wants me to learn how to row but I don't like it. Rowing is hard. The food is ok. Mom. I miss your food. I won't be picky when I come home. Kelly is ok. She does not like to hang out with me. She would rather hang out with her new boyfriend Tyler. He is ugly but Kelly wants to marry him. I think they kissed. I would rather kiss a frog. Dad I hope I marry a boy like you one day. You are more hansome.

Hugs + kisses + hugs + kisses + hugs + kisses + hugs + kisses, Julia [*with a heart on the i*]

Mom/Dad-

I don't have much time tonight and will write more later but don't believe anything Julia tells you. She's a liar. Love,
Kelly

GHOST STORY

"Would you like to hear a ghost story?" He asked.

"Okay," she replied.

"A hundred and fifty years ago there lived a Confederate soldier named Dunlap who lost his sight in the Battle of Fredericksburg. As soon as he was healed enough, he raced home to Cumberland, not too far from here, to be with his wife, Abigail. The only problem was, when he reached home, Abigail was gone. She had disappeared weeks earlier.

"Heartbroken, Dunlap, with a white sash still around his eyes, asked his friend Gus if he would help guide him through the woods in search of her. Gus agreed, and they spent every day searching the woods, shouting her name, 'Abigail! Abigail!'

"Until finally, six months later, an exhausted Gus sat Dunlap down and shared with him what had become the popular opinion in town—that maybe Abigail had simply run away.

"At that moment, Dunlap reached behind his chair, grabbed his rifle, and shot Gus dead in the chest, aiming by the sound of his friend's voice.

"'Abigail would never run away,' he spoke, sealing both of their fates forever.

"After that, no one came to visit Dunlap again. It also meant he had to teach himself how to search the woods alone.

"Now the bigger problem with this was that Abigail had lost her own voice as a child. She had been kicked in the larynx by a horse. She lived her entire adult life as a mute. This meant that if Dunlap were to ever find her, he decided, the only way he could be sure it was her was if they were to kiss.

"And so Dunlap spent the rest of his life—some forty more years before his frozen body was spotted by a local hunter in a ravine—spent them all wandering these woods, shouting the name of his lost love, 'Abigail! Abigail!' hoping one day he would find her and, if he did, be able to kiss her again.

"Of course, everyone thought the story would end there. That was until 1959, when a couple came out nearby here to camp, and the woman described being approached by a young soldier wearing a white sash around his eyes. She said the soldier approached her, yelled 'Abigail!' and kissed her.

"Her boyfriend never heard or saw a thing.

"Over the years, there's been dozens of similar reports—only girls seeing or hearing a blind soldier in the forest yelling 'Abigail!,' then trying to kiss them. And what they've learned is, what you're supposed to do if you happen to be with another guy, you're supposed to say, 'I am not Abigail, I am with the man I love,' before you kiss the guy you're with. That way he knows not to bother you.

"And that's it. That's the story of Dunlap."

"Three things: Number one, I hate you for telling me that story. Number two, don't read any more into what I'm about to do. Number three, I am not Abigail, I am with the man I love."

EMBARRASSED

"You like me, don't you?"

"Yes."

"Then why didn't you come out and say it?"

"It's a little embarrassing."

"What's embarrassing? It's nice."

"I don't know."

"My grandmother use to say that you should never be embarrassed by the things you love. The only person you're embarrassing is yourself. Besides, here's a little secret. I like you, too."

CAPE TOWN

John walked around with his head down
He tripped over a lady in a red night gown
She said, If you believe
Soon you will see
That love can change in an instant

Claire was always staring up at the clouds
Until she backed into a circus clown
He said, If you believe
Soon you will see
That love can change in an instant

Now John was looking up and Claire was looking down
The two biggest fools in this little cape town
Yes, it's hard to believe
Harder still to see
That love can change in an instant

In time we all come around
No harm in falling to the ground
It's hard to believe
She said, at last
That it took so long to see
He said, taking her hand
And now we believe
We've got our whole lives to see
Our love, grow, from this instant

THE EVER AFTER

Prince Hydrant and Lady Citronella sit on the sofa, the rainbow colors of the television pulsing across their expressionless faces. Adorned around them are the many tokens of their union: framed by the door, the front page from The Herald celebrating their wedding (chosen for display specifically by the fact it was the only newspaper *not* to use the words 'Fairy Tale Wedding'), in the far corner (further if she could choose), the sword he used. Above the T.V. compartment, in a glass case, the rose he offered her, still bent at the stem from his overbite and with all but one of the wilted petals since fallen.

The program on the television is a home makeover special detailing steps on how to modernize your centuries old castle without compromising its essence. Prince Hydrant was particularly intrigued by the suggestion that towers make for excellent sundecks. He is still deeply concentrating on whether this would upset the watchmen even as the show moves forward with a tip on how to "Stabilize the Stench of Your Stable."

"I think I'm going to call it an early night," Lady Citronella declares mid-segment.

Prince Hydrant's eyes blink, as if suddenly broken from a spell, and he turns to his everlastingly beautiful bride.

"Goodnight, my love," he speaks, his expression warming with a smile.

"Goodnight, my handsome prince," she returns, leaning in.

"With a kiss," he recites, "a sleep deeper than any poisoned apple could affect."

"That she could be woken by the same in the morning."

"I will. Neither beasts nor bands of knights can stop me, I will."

So this is love, happily in the ever after.

NO USE FOR DREAMING

Fourteen hours earlier they began the process of moving in, filling and unloading a full U-Haul each into their new apartment, their first together. Admittedly, she let him and his two best friends do the heaviest lifting while she directed traffic. They finished near six P.M. and rewarded their helpers with pizza sitting Indian style where the new dining table would soon be. Afterwards, as he returned the truck, she hung the curtains for privacy. By the time he arrived home again, they were too tired to set up the bed and prepared for sleep with the mattress lying flat on the floor. A single goodnight kiss is all he can muster before succumbing to the exhaustion of the day.

Near one A.M. he wakes by the touch of her arm wrapping around him. He rolls over, glad to meet her face so close to his.

"Can't sleep?" He asks.

"Not that, exactly," she says. "I was just thinking. Now that we have this, now that I have you next to me, there's really no more use for dreaming."

WRITING AGAIN

I was writing again. That was the difference. When not writing, time seems to pass like an unstoppable freight train. I am safely on board, but as a passenger, headed wherever the tracks should lead. When writing, it's as if I have the ability to lay the tracks out ahead. Lay them right, and the ninety-seven cars filled with fifty tons cargo each will turn right, reaching Boston by daylight. Lay them left, and this locomotive will pass through the Rockies by midweek. Tonight, I lay them straight ahead. Towards Cincinnati, because that is where she is. And in the morning I will arrive, with ninety-seven cars, loaded fifty tons each, filled with rose petals for her to place wherever her feet should reach.

THE GIRL

You know what that means, right? The girl. Like, not the girl you crushed on for a little while in eighth grade, but *the* girl. The one that never left you from the start, from the day you first met her; the girl that, and this is probably unfair to her, but, the one that makes you feel like, you, or at least a better you. She inspires you to do all the right things, makes you do the right things—'cause that's it, as long as you're living with her in mind, it's gotta be the right thing. Which is why it hurts so much when she's not there, living without her. Then it feels like going down the wrong path, further away from her, wrong. And I guess that's the heart of it, what makes her *the* girl—that as complicated as life can be sometimes, she simplifies it: When she's there, it's okay; and when she's not, it's doing everything you can to be near her again. At least, that's all you'll ever want. Does that make sense?"

"Yes. But why?"

"'Cause it's you. For me anyway, for as long as I've known you, you've been the girl."

ODE TO A PEPPERMINT PATTY

Oh, if you only knew the strength I kept to steel myself for each visit by one of those gluttonous monsters with the leering eyes. How they surveyed us individually only to belittle us all with the blunt use of that most insolent of words, "snack." As if we exist only to fulfill a small craving, a bridge before something better; that we are not each masterpieces ourselves.

And on this discussion of masterpieces, there is but one. One who belongs where the world's treasures are kept, one whose existence transcended what it is to be a candy or a confection—not the key to a heart, but as if the very heart itself. She was, my heart, wrapped in silver cellophane.

Heavens, the evening she arrived into my life! B3, for as long as I knew, had been home to the brazenly twisted families and relatives of licorice. They were all in a single day moved aside, replaced by a row of sisters unmatched on this Earth: Twelve ladies who, in daylight, reflected like twelve high noon suns, or at night, gleamed like a dozen twinkling stars in our boxed twilight.

Yes, days and nights, nights and days—this is what became of my life. A constant dueling of happiness and despair while time forever shortened.

Days, of course, being the epitome of despair: Torturous, ten-hour intervals, grinding myself to crumbs with each selection. Nearly unmentionable, the outright horror with every instance her number was chosen, when the great wheels would spin and she would glide further and further away from view, all while my brothers and I remained still, my back seemingly forever to the wall.

But nights, glorious nights, when I knew she was safe. When her view remained constant, her profile, iridescent in the dark. Those nights I lived forever. I would stay awake, prolonging that feeling of peace, delaying the abrupt flash of a fluorescent morning, when a lifetime would be taken from me once more.

How perfect those nights were! Ask the Pop-Tarts! Inquire to the Funyuns! The Doublemints will know. They witnessed: my salt and her sweet. They heard our conversations at night; our laughter, echoing through the chamber, sending vibrations through the machine. They felt our love. They knew it filled a void no hunger can reach.

But, alas, how short our time was meant to be. This was an ending any simple treat could foresee. Unlike my brothers, she shined too bright, her sweet, too sweet.

And now, see right through me: my almond will, no longer shelled; my raisin heart, weathered but pure. See me here, if you'd like, as a snack with my back still to the wall. But I know what I saw, the way she glistened, even as she was led away. I saw her glisten, and I have no doubt, she glistened for me.

CASUAL DATING

"You seeing anyone these days?"
"Well, I was casually dating for a while."
"What happened?"
"I found out there's no such thing as casual."
"I'm sorry, did some girl break your heart?"
"The opposite. She put it back together."

GIRL

It's a girl. We found an anomaly. She's in our prayers. I can't lose her. She's perfect. Look, she's got your eyes. What's her name? That's my thithter. Amazing, she never cries. How's grandma's little munchkin? She better have my genes because all she ever wants to do is eat. Uhp, there she goes again. You get that picture? The tests all came up negative. I hate her! Maybe we should buy her a chew toy. What if she gets scared? She discovered ice cream. I've never seen him sleep like that, only when he's next to her. How's grandma's little munchkinbunchkin? She's over here, they found a mud pit. Plays well with others. I think your daughter stole my son's Hot Wheel. That she got from you. Two cavities on her left side. For our next trick: Disappearing sister! Twenty-nine stitches. Participates. One call from Braughton Associates, and seven messages from your daughter. We baked a nine-layer cake. Don't get upset, but she painted a daisy on your car with nail polish. Energetic. Brownies, welcome your fathers to your very first lock-in! Lindsey just adores her. So polite! Scored two goals before she kicked that Polly girl again. Excels in math, could focus more on reading. How's grandma's little munchkinbunch-kin satonhertumskin? I found all her books hidden in the woodshed—which she said, by the way, you wouldn't find because you hardly ever cut the lawn. Should really be brushing more, less candy, too. What do you mean she's too old for that? She's a little homesick. Perfect attendance. Isn't she turning in to just the most beautiful little lady? It's a broken nose; that little witch number four aimed it right at her face. You know what they say: For those who can't sing, God invented drums. We'll be right back, girl issues. I think she has a boyfriend. It's just three hours, he's her favorite singer, you'll be fine. Can she babysit every night? Are you aware of the fingertip test? They broke up. Second Team All-State. Fractured fifth metatarsal. Listen honey, I know you don't believe in pure evil, but you weren't ever a teenage girl either. Three A's, three C's. Her teacher said it was the first time he felt bad about giving detention for punching. Learner's permit. This year's winner of Battle of the Bands: The Whatevs. Don't tell her this, but I kind of miss her. 1480! Tattoo? That's three thousand miles away! I promise to have her back by ten. "…would like to offer you a partial athletic scholarship." Aly's parents invited her to Spain after graduation. Most Talented. But what if she never wants to come back? Hi, yes, my name is Nick De Lucci, our daughters room together, and I've just learned they've been booked for underage drinking in Portland, Oregon. Oh my God, she got a 4.0. Whew, he says EDM is a type of music. She's bringing someone home for Thanksgiving. Her e-mail says you can download the song on the inter-net if you search for 'Kick Polly.' She's furious, she got a 3.9. Her roommate has leukemia. You'll never believe it, she just called, she wants to be a doctor. Can we pay for Med School? I think he might be the one. Boston's not far, at least. Salutatorian. It's okay, I'm nearby, I'll look after her. There's something I'd like to ask you. Don't worry dear, we'll have leftovers for the next six months, this is the dress. I'm so proud of my little munchkin bunchkin ooooh isn't she going to be the most gorgeous brideschkin! Can't we go back; I'm not ready to stop being her mother. And who gives this woman away?

THE RIGHT FIT

I'm here to tell you right now, if you're looking for someone to run away with, if you think you need a different adventure every day, I'm here to tell you: I love you, and I wish you every adventure you could ever dream of, but they won't be with me. It wouldn't be fair to you to pretend.

But if you're looking for someone to run home to, if you think there's enough adventure already in life without chasing it, and you want someone to be your rock—I'll be that for you. That's what I'm good at. I'm real good at being strong; I'm real good at taking away the worry. With me, you'll never have to worry.

The truth is, we're going to love each other either way. I know that. It just also happens to be the truth that some loves fit better than others. I want ours to be the right fit.

CLOVER FIELD

Don't throw your love in a wishing well
What comes back no one can tell
You have control
You have control

You threw your love in a wishing well
Here I am, did it work out well?
You have control
You have control

The water hits the windowsill
Who's that waiting on the hill?
You have control
You have control

A rainbow lands in a clover field
You're standing there, my heart is still
I have found love
I have found love

SUNRISE

None of the others managed to stay awake. They all petered out at separate intervals, finishing with Jamie, who had been the most gung ho throughout the night, only to succumb to the bowl chair sometime after three.

So he ironed himself for the solo trip, making coffee at four-thirty and sitting through an infomercial until five. At five-fifteen, he grabbed his Quicksilver hoodie and marched out. Though the street was empty, he could still hear the echoes of the night in his ears. Turn the clock only four hours back and the carnival was still passing through. Now there was silence.

Where the pavement ended, he removed his sandals and felt the cool sand beneath his feet. In five hours, they would all congregate here again, with their coolers and towels and chairs, ready to ogle at their own roasting bodies one last time.

The beach appeared empty. Earlier in the season there would have been others, perhaps five or six or more, but it was late August now. Most had seen their single sunrise for the year and would be content to see winter pass before waking again.

He never could get enough, though, especially knowing that no two mornings were ever the same. Sometimes the sun would spring from the ocean's edge like it had bounced from a ringing toaster. Other times, it sat and fried like an egg on the horizon. And, of course, that rare treat, always to be wished for—the fabled green flash...

She woke at four-forty-five, stretched until five, and had already completed two dark miles when she reached him. In any other instance she would have kept on running (you run far enough and there's bound to be someone out there) but something struck her as incredibly sincere, if not slightly sad, at the way he had held his hand out to her in a motionless wave.

"Excuse me," he said. "I know this might sound a little strange, but I was hoping you might watch with me. It'll be up any minute."

She stopped entirely as he turned to face the sea. After a curious minute of catching her breath and observing him, she felt comfortable enough to stand alongside him and dug her burning toes into the sand where the tireless waves nearly reached. Moments later, when the very end of the sky flashed a pale green, she felt she understood why he had wanted her here with him. Felt as if she understood completely.

WAIT

"Wait."

"What's the matter?"

"I didn't say everything I meant to say. I mean, I thought we had so much time. I thought I'd have plenty of time. But I feel like I'm running out and I haven't said everything I wanted to say."

"What did you want to say?"

"I love you. I wanted to say I love you."

THE ATRIUM

The man enters the bodega at 12:15 exactly. He is frail, and though he attempts to stand tall, his left leg drags. We cannot always help that our parts do not move as well as our mind.

He purchases a half bottle of wine, a loaf of bread, and a small block of cheese. After paying in exact change, he delivers a courteous "Thank you," and steps out again, his left foot dragging.

On Seventh Street, he boards the #18 bus. The younger passengers make room for him by the door. He observes them with a wishful smile, admiring the important business that awaits them. He had business like that once, but that was long ago. His business is of a different sort now.

He departs only nine blocks north, at the base of Juniper Lane's long hill. Help has been offered before, but he climbs alone, to the very top of the rise where he turns right into the park.

The old atrium is there, first built in 1919. For years it had served as a bandstand as well as the site of late evening romantic activities too numerous to count. In 1970, a second, larger atrium was built down by the pond and now the smaller atrium stands nearly forgotten.

Perhaps that is why he chooses it, or maybe his cataracts trouble him too much to notice the cutting branches of leafless ivy, the flower beds overrun by weeds.

He spreads his picnic on the center bench and waits, sometimes a few minutes, other times an hour. He does not mind that she is less punctual. If he had a better leg, he would pause longer to admire certain things, too.

Arrive, she does, however, taking a seat opposite the man, and placing two stemmed glasses between them. Soon they share their familiar toast, "To good health and good company," which every time elicits a broad smile from them both. They know full well the value of each.

So it is that they spend their Monday and Thursday afternoons, in the old atrium at the high end of the park. No, parts do not always work as well as they should, but some parts are sturdier than others.

LIGHT THE WAY

Did you go to sleep thinking
The moon would lie in wait?
Or did you wake up hoping
The sun would last all day?

Of all the lessons to impart
Let this be the one that stays:
There is no lonely in the dark
When love lights your way.

A NEW HOBBY

Jackie returned from her morning jog to find a thin stream of water trickling down the length of her driveway. She felt her stomach sink as she traced the glistening trail to the center of her garage door, where no doubt the brand new forty-gallon water heater had to be the leaking culprit. At least it wasn't in the basement, she thought.

Reaching for the automatic door's keypad, she heard a roar from inside that sounded like a chainsaw, buzzing even louder than the running mix blaring through her headphones.

She punched the four-digit code and jumped five steps back, prepared to run if need be.

When the door opened, she found her husband in khaki shorts and sandals, holding an actual chainsaw, beside a giant block of ice that might have been in the shape of a heart—or at least, if that's what it was supposed to be, the upper right curl had fallen off.

"Hi honey," he said, beaming.

She had no words.

The toy trains. That was one thing. She never said a word about those stupid toy trains. But ice sculpturing? This wasn't part of the bargain.

"Here, come closer. Look right here. Chiseled it myself."

She shuffled closer, avoiding his chainsaw side.

"Is that my name?" She asked, seeing the letters crudely chipped into the ice with the kind of block type mental patients use in movies. The c in particular was an overlarge < shape that looked like it wanted to eat the k.

"Yes!"

"All right, fine. Do you really want me to ask?"

"Yes, I do," still beaming.

"Okay. Why, honey, have you decided to sculpt a heart, out of ice, with my name on it, using a chainsaw, in our garage?"

"I wanted to see if I could melt your heart."

THE VILLAGE SLEEPS

She speaks to me, though I have not seen her face, nor heard her voice.

I had come close tonight. Or at least the air of possibility seemed more prominent. With each change in venue—a celebration on the Upper East Side, a rooftop in Murray Hill, karaoke in Alphabet City, and here, the after-after party within an alley-facing apartment on Bleecker St.— the hope seemed to rise, that something extraordinary were near to happening.

Extraordinary requires the unexpected, and tonight, if nothing else, had been unexpected.

Through the small square window, the glow of morning can no longer be doubted. The never ending night has ended. As the shades draw down on my too-worthy companions, I escape to the empty streets.

The change is distinguishable. It is as if the neighborhood were an instrument finely tuned to the daylight. The sun rises and The Village sleeps.

Not everyone. On Bedford St., I pass a model in a silver sequin dress. Her frozen pose suggests she had been wrong to trust a careless photographer. So she stands, waiting for a flash that will never come. A block away, two young Spanish men descend into a restaurant's cellar, exchanging empty kegs for full ones.

It is cold, I realize, a late summer chill. I pass a twenty-four hour diner and find shelter inside, feeling my stomach wake.

"Good morning, sweethawt," greets my waitress, Carla. She is fiftyish, her accent is buttery thick and sweet in an almost too loving sort of way. I am her first customer. She is going to take good care of me, she says, filling my coffee "nice and high."

As Carla turns away, I begin to think of the girl again. I can hear her, as if she sits across from me at this very table.

"Are you tired?" She asks.

"Yes," I say.

"It's not easy, is it?" She continues.

"No, it is not."

"But it will be worth it, won't it, when you find me?"

"Yes. Yes it will be."

The Village sleeps. Somewhere, she does, too. It is cold again outside and I know this is only part of the story, a prelude. The best parts will come soon.

THE DEBATE

"...and that's why I hope to get your vote this afternoon. Thank you."

"Very good, June. Now, Michael, your turn, if you would like to share why you think you should represent your classmates as Class President."

"Thank you, Mrs. Conner. And thank you, June—I'm going to come back to you in a second, but right now I just want to say that running against you has been an honor and a privilege. So thank you.

"What can I say? These last few weeks have been a total blast. Your support has been awesome, and I owe a special shout out to Wogie and Burt who nearly got arrested trying to help me out—that rally at the lake was ridiculous and I feel like I'm going to owe you guys the rest of my life.

"These three weeks have been productive, too. We laid out a plan for the South Fields, we're gonna get better lunch privileges in January, and I have to wait to tell you the news, but there's a big surprise coming for Prom that you're all really gonna like.

"Which brings me back to this election. And June. I understand a lot of you don't know June too well. She moved here just this summer. That took a lot of guts for her to run. I hope this election has helped you to get to know her better.

"I also think that if you're going to be voting today, it might help to know who we, as candidates, will be voting for. The answer, for me anyway, is June.

"Two reasons. First, and more important for you all to know, is she would be a better president than me, in nearly every single possible way. And the second reason, and I'm sorry to put you on the spot here June, but I feel like I have to say it: I'm completely in love with you."

IN THE ZONE

I am on my backside looking up. The stadium lights are actually bunches of eight lights each, arranged in two rows of four. The second from the left on the bottom row seems directed like a spotlight at me, creating a sort of halo in my vision. It is strangely quiet. I wonder if I am so far In The Zone that I no longer hear distraction. I *am* in the end zone, I believe. I recall crossing the line of white chalk while somersaulting, which I did do, somersault, like being in one of those Space Camp contraptions that spin on three axes at once, only I was not strapped in. I am all but positive the crossing of the chalked goal line occurred in a forward motion, meaning I must be very deep In The Zone to not now hear a celebration. The halo breaks and Gunther is above me, covering half the light with a look of extreme reinforcement on his face while nodding his head vigorously up and down. "Yes, Gunther, a touchdown is good," I think to say, helping him along. Motion on my right causes me to turn my head. I see vomiting. A mixture of which, by team that is: Bo and Igor in white and what looks to be most of the aqua-jerseyed Henderson D-line, in unison, like an elaborate five-spigot fountain designed in the shape of bloated porpoises, all of them, vomiting. I assume Bo and Igor's ills are in reaction to Henderson's squad who must have first gotten sick by my having been so very much In The Zone, catapulting, cartwheeling no doubt into the homes of each of their dear friends and relatives who will see my highlight again on their 11 P.M. news and inevitably hit rewind over and over in majestic awe of my Zoneness. Now Coach is above me, disrupting the halo again. When he speaks, only his lower teeth show. I have never seen his upper teeth, only his lower teeth which appear as a single giant ivory horseshoe of enamel. He is also nodding. I try to raise the football in accordance but my arm does not cooperate. The Zone is deep and pure. "You do not enter The Zone," Coach teaches us, "The Zone enters you." There is something tiresome about watching Coach's seamless row of bottom teeth move and not being able to hear what he is saying. I turn my head away. The cheerleaders seem to be in prayer, a dance I have never seen them perform before. Broken from them, however, is Piper, running towards me now, her legs like an antelope bearing white socks and our school letters jostling rhythmically across her top. In a moment she is above me, too, and the halo lands about her small face just right, just the way it should, and I think I'll tell her how beautiful she looks with a halo perfectly centered around her face, and she dips down and kisses me, and I feel a pulse of warmth rush through me, unlike any Zone I have experienced before, so far In It I am now, deeply In The Zone, and she is In The Zone with me, and together we are In and Of at once within this Zone of all Zones and I think I should reach up and hold her closer so that we can be exactly One in this Heavenly Zone when all the sounds of the stadium return in a rush and I hear her say, "Just look at me, don't look d—"

MASTERPIECE

I wrote something beautiful
And my wish came true
They called it a masterpiece
Not knowing, it was you

AU REVOIR

Though he sits on a bench in New York City, he is far away. This must be the Seine, not the East River, and in a proper world, that would be the Eiffel Tower gleaming in place of the 59th Street Bridge. It is so much easier to believe in love when there is still time, he thinks. He remembers how they had stayed awake in defense of just that, slowing time. So long as they had another moment to grasp, one final second to stretch endlessly, they might discover eternity does exist. But now there are only memoires of those final hours—of her awake and Paris asleep, the four A.M. courtesy call crashing the aura of an infinite night, and, at last, her final "Au revoir," whispered from the end of a serpentine security line within Charles de Gaulle. "Until we see again," he answered her, understanding the promise within such a literal translation. No simple farewell could ever do...

"Don't you remember?" She speaks. Her dress is the color of the sun. He knows this before he turns. "We met once, in New York, three, maybe four years ago. Then again, in Paris, just five days ago. And what I distinctly remember is falling in love."

WHAT REMAINS

In Philadelphia, a man kisses a girl and her heel rises. In Charlotte, under a blanket tent, twin sisters shout at the count of three the name of the same boy they both like. In Iowa City, a mother nurses her three-day old son for the first time totally alone. "Twenty years from now," she says, "if you don't have a date on a Saturday night, remember me, okay?" In San Diego, a grandmother takes her granddaughter shopping for a new dress. The dress they choose is an inch-and-a-half shorter than her mother would have let her wear. In Austin, an eight year old boy kisses a nine year old girl. "That's not how you do it," she says, "but you can try again." In Portland, two men recite their vows. The church erupts in hysterics when the second declares "Yes," in place of "I do." In Charleston, best friends cling together for the first time in nineteen years. There are scars between them that may never heal, but apart never did much to heal those either. In St. Cloud, a couple watches the news together. They hear a story of a dog that traveled 1,100 miles to reunite with its owner. They laugh, in part because it is miraculous, but also because the husband had once traveled twice as far. In Philadelphia, two octogenarians witness a girl lower her heel again. So much has changed in their lifetimes, but the best things remain the same.

THE END

She said, "I liked your story, and I believe you love me…"

"Then what is it?" He asked.

"I don't want it to end."

"It never ends," he replied.

"But all stories end."

"You asked me to write you a love story," he said. "And love stories never end."

WITH LOVE

I am often asked whether the stories I write are real or not. The simple answer is that the stories are, of course, fiction. They are built like little houses each and the details of any setting, action, or plot are on the scale of determining which color to paint the exterior or whether to add a bay window to the front or not. What is closer to real, however, are the emotions. This is the light within each house, illuminated by the families, friends, and loves that make each house a home.

It is true that no book is written alone. If I was able to build a neighborhood of 260 homes, it was only because I had family, friends, and even loves offer their own dedication, their own inspiration, their support, their warmth, plenty of patience, an endless supply of joy, and an ever fortunately small dose of sadness to carry with me. In short, in their infinite ways, words, and gestures, they offered me their love.

So thank you, to each of you who played a part. Let's write many more stories together.

With love,
Rich

ABOUT THE AUTHOR

Rich Walls graduated from Villanova University in 2006 and published his first novel, *Standby, Chicago*, in 2011. He presently lives in Hoboken, New Jersey.

Follow future installments of One Page Love Story at:

www.onepagelovestory.com

93033111R00148

Made in the USA
Columbia, SC
08 April 2018